KALIDASA

Praise for *Kalidasa*

'Poet Mani Rao is Kalidasa's new cloud-messenger. Sharp and concise in her renditions, she makes Kalidasa's works live and breathe linguistically in our own time. In the process she creates, with rare skill, a new lyricism, makes the terse speak with unusual depth and feeling. As we go further away from our inheritances, translations like Rao's will help open up the extraordinary multiverse that is our past.'

—SHARMISTHA MOHANTY

'Mani Rao's translations of Kalidasa are enormously respectful of the great poetry of the original and also enjoyable for their contemporary interventions and segues into our times. This is a must-read for anyone who is interested in poetry, drama, translation and Indic literary traditions.'

—JERRY PINTO

'Mani Rao's *Kalidasa* adds her own poetic voice to his classic works as she pulls them firmly forward into our times. She is neither afraid nor in awe of the texts she translates and renews them for all of us to enjoy. Rao's work, here and elsewhere, shows us that a classic can never be exhausted by multiple translations, it can only be enriched.'

—ARSHIA SATTAR

KALIDASA

SELECTED POETRY & DRAMA

TRANSLATED FROM THE SANSKRIT BY

MANI RAO

HarperCollins *Publishers* India

First published in India by HarperCollins *Publishers* 2025
HarperCollins *Publishers* India, Cyber City,
Building 10-A, Gurugram, Haryana – 122002, India
www.harpercollins.co.in

2 4 6 8 10 9 7 5 3 1

P-ISBN: 978-93-6989-520-5
E-ISBN: 978-93-6989-662-2

Typeset in 10.5/14 Times New Roman
by HarperCollins *Publishers* India Pvt. Ltd

Printed and bound at
Thomson Press (India) Ltd

MIX
Paper | Supporting responsible forestry
FSC® C010615

This book is produced from independently certified FSC® paper
to ensure responsible forest management.

HarperCollins *Publishers*, Macken House, 39/40 Mayor Street Upper,
Dublin 1, D01 C9W8, Ireland

TRANSLATOR'S DEDICATION

Kālī Ma
Tongue unshy
Your necklace chatters
Tassles sigh
Mercy, Kālī

Everyone's Ma
Nobody's Lover
Sister Daughter
Slaughter

CONTENTS

Introduction
ix

How to Pronounce Diacritics
xvi

MEGHADŪTAM
Cloud-Messenger
1

ABHIJÑĀNA ŚĀKUNTALAM
Śakuntalā's Souvenir
57

ṚTUSAṂHĀRAM
A Collection of Seasons
187

RAGHUVAṂŚAM
The Raghu Dynasty
201

KUMĀRASAMBHAVAM
The Birth of Kumāra
231

MĀLAVIKĀGNIMITRAM
Mālavikā and Agnimitra
265

VIKRAMORVAŚĪYAM
Heroism Wins Urvaśī
289

INTRODUCTION

Indian Poetry's Genius

Popular legends describe Kālidāsa's transformation from fool to genius. One day, this fool sits on a tree in the wrong spot, about to chop the very branch he sits upon, and is noticed by the king's minister who holds a grudge against the kingdom's princess. The minister gives the fool a makeover, presents him at court as an erudite prince and succeeds in marrying him off to the gullible princess. When the princess finds out the truth, she abandons the fool at the local Kālī temple. The fool's simplicity and devotion win over Goddess Kālī, who writes upon his tongue and transforms him into a brilliant poet. Thereafter, this fool is called Kālidāsa, 'devoted servant of Kālī'. The legend is telling; that only a divine intervention can create such talent reveals to us just how highly Kālidāsa is regarded by posterity.

The miraculous transformation from fool to genius also makes the poet endearing rather than formidable. A Sanskrit verse illustrates Kālidāsa's place as the foremost among poets with a humorous story around counting by hand. In the old Indian way of counting on a hand, the palm faced up and the little finger got tallied first. Once, when poets were being counted, the first to be counted, on the little finger, was Kālidāsa. The next in line was the ring finger, but there was no other poet who could follow Kālidāsa … Naturally, this finger was anāmikā, which means 'nameless'.

Kālidāsa's poems and plays made a strong impression on centuries of Indian publics, poets and critics. One may find arguments about the exact reason for Kālidāsa's towering status in Sanskrit literature, but rarely any negative criticism or disagreement about his status.

The twelfth-century poet Jayadeva called Kālidāsa 'the guru of the family of poets'. Treatises on Sanskrit poetics turn so often to lines from Kālidāsa's poems and plays for examples of figures of speech and use of metre, it seems as if Kālidāsa's compositions literally shaped the ars poetica of Sanskrit literature and dramatics. Examples from across Kālidāsa's poems and plays can fill an entire book on the śṛṅgāra rasa, the erotic emotion of Indian poetics. But if Kālidāsa has a knack for śṛṅgāra, he also knows of complications when duty clashes with desire. Kālidāsa's literary skill is matched by his knowledge of human nature and ability to observe. Touching moments in the play *Abhijñāna Śākuntalam*, and the poems *Raghuvaṃśam* and *Meghadūtam* show a compassionate understanding of emotional states. *Śākuntalam* and *Ṛtusaṃhāram*, and even *Kumārasambhavam*, show a sensitivity to the lively beauty in nature; when Kālidāsa compares the physical beauty of women to natural objects, the compliment seems directed to nature. *Mālavikāgnimitram* and *Vikramorvaśīyam* show a sympathy for obsessive love along with an understanding of love-politics.

Kālidāsa's metrical skill is impeccable. Technical choices, for sure, create related effects—in *Meghadūtam*, the mandākrānta metre of seventeen syllabic lines creates a slow, meandering rhythm, apt for the cloud's voyage. But Kālidāsa works with the metre so deftly that the reader never feels that a word is contrived, or chosen for its syllable length or phonetic features rather than for aptness of meaning and suggestion. There is a lot of information in the long lines of *Meghadūtam*, but each detail informs the other, and it all adds up to more than the sum of the parts. The antelope runs to avoid the rain; meanwhile the earth responds to the same rain, and the antelope sniffs the rising fragrance … What we have is a montage—all these things come together at once.

Life and Times

'Who is Kālidāsa?' is a perplexing question. We do not know when and where Kālidāsa lived, in what kingdom or era, who his parents were, or his contemporaries, nor even if his name is a pseudonym. This prolific poet did not write about himself directly. Rājaśekhara, a tenth-century poet known for his figures of speech, noted that Kālidāsa remained unbeatable. Seventh-century CE writer Bāṇabhaṭṭa praised the delights of Kālidāsa's poetry in his poem-chronicle *Harṣacarita*. Seventh-century CE philosopher Kumārila Bhaṭṭa cited from Kālidāsa's play *Śākuntalam*. An inscription at Aihole, dated 634 AD, mentions Kālidāsa by name, along with the poet Bhāravi. That, then, gives us an estimate of when he was born, that Kālidāsa lived before the early seventh century CE. The upper limit is less easy to fix. One source names Kālidāsa, along with eight others, as one of the nine gems of King Vikrama's court. But we do not know if there was more than one Kālidāsa, nor exactly who King Vikrama was—'vikrama' could simply be an appellation that means 'victorious'. One King Vikramāditya defeated the Śakas and established the Samvat Era that began in the first century BCE; another Vikramāditya was King Yaśodharman, who defeated the Hūṇas in the sixth century CE. Yet another Vikramāditya was the Gupta king, Chandragupta II, who ruled from Ujjayinī in the fourth century CE.

Perhaps identity is best answered by citing works, but it's complicated when over thirty works can be attributed to Kālidāsa. Over the centuries, works most often cited as Kālidāsa's are the four poems and three plays included in this volume, with some lack of consensus about the authorship of the poem *Ṛtusaṃhāram*. The poem *Meghadūtam* and the play *Abhijñāna Śākuntalam*, are translated in full. A substantial excerpt has been translated from the other works: an act each from the plays *Mālavikāgnimitram* and *Vikramorvaśīyam*, a canto each from the poems *Kumārasambhavam* and *Raghuvaṃśam*, and selected stanzas from each of the six sections of *Ṛtusaṃhāram*. Studying these seven works gives us an idea of the depth of Indian poetry's heritage, early Indian aesthetic values, as well as helps us reimagine life in early India of around the fourth century CE.

Appreciating Kālidāsa, Translating Kālidāsa

Today, if most people know the storylines of Kālidāsa's famous works *Śākuntalam* and *Meghadūtam*, not as many have actually read them, even in translation. This is unsurprising, for the conventions of ancient Indian poetics are far removed from our present context. We no longer compare women's faces to lotuses or their figures to vines, and fanciful expressions of love just seem obsessive-compulsive. And because translations just cannot replicate Kālidāsa's metre, the English-language reader cannot relish his literary delights. However, those who read Kālidāsa in Sanskrit know that his brilliance is not just in prosody; it is in the use of the apt word, in the suggestiveness and unity of parts, how everything comes together. This kind of literary appreciation is one of the goals of this translation. A couple of examples will help illustrate the methodology.

In *Meghadūtam*, we learn that the hero, a supernatural being called a yakṣa, lived on a mountain named Rāmagiri. Why is the mountain called Rāmagiri? Kālidāsa does not spell it out, nor do any commentators. In fact, 'Rāmagiri' has unmistakable connotations for anyone who knows something about the importance of the epic Rāmāyaṇa in the Indian imagination. The anguish felt by the yakṣa upon this mountain recalls the anguish of Rāma when separated from Sītā. The cloud (megha) brings back thoughts of Hanumān, who is the son of the god of wind, flies like a cloud, and is Rāma's messenger (dūta). A comment within the translation (see p. 5) helps the reader pay attention to these connotations. And what kind of hero is this yakṣa? The first word in the poem is 'some' (kaścit)—we are about to enter an epic-length poem from Kālidāsa, and the character we meet is nondescript. This is most unusual. In the very first line, we are told of the yakṣa's lapse of duty. Unless the reader knows the context of classical poetry and what is expected of heroes about whom poems are written, they will not realize its significance. A duty or obligation (adhikāra) is the same as privilege (adhikāra). Therefore, those who neglect their duty are not rebels; they are foolish, they are giving up their privileges. Has the yakṣa become ordinary after the curse? Was it because he was besotted? An anti-hero? This translation helps point out this contrast by way of a commentarial remark. But it does not spoil all the fun. Why the use of the plural in 'hermitages'? A wandering yakṣa, lost soul? Kālidāsa does not say, nor do I. Having expanded just a little, I get back to Kālidāsa's summary-style brevity, repeating the 'story so far' and then move to the next narrative step.

Across this translation, such commentarial input also takes the form of word choices, translation decisions. An example is in the dedication of *Raghuvaṃśam*. Kālidāsa compares Śiva and Pārvatī to speech (vāc) and meaning: 'Vāgarthāviva sampṛktau vāgarthapratipattaye, Jagataḥ pitarau vande pārvatīparameśvarau.' This stanza is popular as a stand-alone devotional hymn. It is also often quoted in discussions around language and Indian theories of meaning, and as an example of a poet seeking inspiration and divine help. M.R. Kale translates in *The Raghuvamsa* (1957): 'For the right comprehension of words and their senses, I salute Parvati (the mountain's daughter) and Paramesvara (the supreme Lord), the parents of the universe who are (perpetually) united like words and their meanings' (p. 125). The meaning of the Sanskrit verse is conveyed accurately in Kale's literal translation. I go a little further. I translate: 'To make words meaningful / I invoke Śiva–Pārvatī // Makers of the world / Like word and meaning wed.' By saying 'makers' instead of parents, and also using the word 'make' for what the poet does, I draw attention to their connection.

In general, I try to recapture the effect rather than the arrangements of the parts. In *Meghadūtam*, I often repeat a phrase that applies to several parts of the stanza, gaining the sense of an oral rendition, as well as the montage effect. *Raghuvaṃśam* has a different pace: more brisk and compact. In the first canto translated here, each stanza has a distinct concept—an analogy, or a pattern—that adds to the narrative. On a cursory reading, stanzas 6, 7 and 8, which talk about the ideal king, may seem random, but they have tight, logical links. In fact, Stanza 6 is about the extent of the Raghu dynasty, its influence. Dative case governs stanza 7; it informs us about the purpose of kings and their high motivations, and this contrasts with the worldly supremacy we learned about in stanza 6. Stanza 8 covers their propriety, and within four lines we find out how the Raghu kings behave in each of their life-stages. Stanzas 7 and 8, therefore, build on the information given in Stanza 6. I indicate these connections by adding 'yet' and 'and', words which are not in the original. Everywhere, such interpolations, whether for the purpose of appreciation, or for explanation, are indicated by italicization and indentation. This method also helps do away with footnotes or endnotes altogether, and minimal explanatory remarks are integrated into the rhythm of the translated text for an uninterrupted reading. Where I have explained names, or given more recognizable names to descriptors or epithets, I have not used italics—thus, Śaphara 'fish', 'river' Gambhīrā, 'three-eyed' Śiva, 'Śiva's consort' Bhavānī, fire-born 'Skanda', oblation-bearer 'god of fire, Agni'. However, for expressions that involve an imaginative usage, or where I draw attention to an etymology, I italicize my interpolations—thus, cowherd guise *Kṛṣṇa*, *fragrant river* Gandhavatī.

In Kālidāsa's plays (and other ancient Sanskrit plays), characters are often denoted by their roles: King, Jester, Attendant, and so on. This is also in line with how names tend to be descriptive; thus, Nipuṇikā means attendant and skilful, Anasūyā is free of jealousy, Priyaṃvadā is sweet-spoken, and so on. And in service to fidelity, translators automatically translate 'rājā' as 'king', 'vidūṣaka' as 'jester', 'sūta' as 'charioteer' and 'kañcukī' as 'chamberlain'. This becomes disorientating for modern readers and casting directors. When every attendant is called 'attendant', how many attendants does one need to cast? Groups of people are often indicated by a word like 'sa-parivāra' (with family, i.e., with entourage). For instance: Enter the daughter of the King of Kāśī, with her entourage (sa-parivārā). Asks the casting director: How many?

Why is Śakuntalā always called 'Śakuntalā', but Duṣyanta only ever referred to as 'King'? Is this a subconscious deference to male authority, or is it that there is only one king? If the king knows the name of the attendant, why can't the readers and the audience? The modern mind seeks out individuality and personalities via names. The jesters in the three plays here (Mādhavya, Māṇavaka and Gautama) have distinctive personalities (and there is an essay idea here for a student), and *within* the dialogues, other characters know and address them by their names. Therefore, in my translation, the jester's role is defined the first time they are mentioned (such as Mādhavya, the jester); subsequently, Mādhavya is called 'Mādhavya'.

Occasionally, where Kālidāsa does not give the person a name, I retain the Sanskrit descriptor. Thus, the king calls his chamberlain Kañcukī in this translation, which is also more natural, or just ethnic, on stage than the king saying—'Chamberlain, carry on with your work' (which sounds simply contrived).

While Kālidāsa's poetry has metrical craftsmanship and intricate design, and features colourful similes, it is also attentive, precise, purposeful—values of modernist poetry. Whereas the plays cover a range of locations, shift between human and divine realms, they can also zoom in on fine details of emotional states. In addition to showing how Kālidāsa can speak to contemporary poetics, I also use contemporary language. Thus, in the plays, I use language which today's actors may speak comfortably on stage. No quaint addresses like 'Hail, Majesty' to King Duṣyanta, nor the address 'friend' when speaking to a person the audience already knows is a friend. As we enter the world of Kālidāsa, Kālidāsa's world also enters ours.

HOW TO PRONOUNCE DIACRITICS

For the most part, Sanskrit diacritics are used in this translation for proper names. The guide below is not comprehensive, but ought to help you say most of the names correctly. Basic tips: A dash over a vowel makes it a longer syllable. Curl your tongue back when there is a dot under the letter, except for ṃ, ḥ and ṛ (see chart below for those). The letter h after consonants calls for aspiration, or an outbreath.

Vowels:

a as in u in cut
ā as in father
i as in bit
ī as in beet
u as in put or foot
ū as in brute or cool
e as in bay or fate
ai as in sigh or aisle
o as in hope
au as in sound or flautist
ṛ (which is a vowel in Sanskrit) similar to brunch, or rig
ṃ nasalize the preceding vowel so that oṃ as in the French bon
ḥ softly echoes the preceding vowel

Consonants: as for English except for

v as wall
ś as shame (whereas s as in so)
ṣ similar to dish
c as church or chutney

t as pasta

ṅ as sung

ñ as canyon

ṇ has no equivalent in English, but it is a retroflex, the tongue needs to curl backwards to touch the palate and then hit the back of the teeth

d as in the

ḍ as in dart

kh, gh, ch, jh, th, dh, ph, bh are aspirated consonants, the h is pronounced along with an outbreath. This sound has no exact equivalent in English, but the following examples will help approximate the sound. Thus, k as in skate but kh similar to Khan; g as in gate but gh as in the country, Ghana; ch as in much honey; and so on. Thus: yakṣa is pronounced yuck-sh(as dish)-u(as but).

MEGHADŪTAM

Cloud-Messenger

In *Meghadūtam*, a yakṣa, who is a supernatural being, requests a cloud to carry a message of love and longing to his lover who is far away. The yakṣa hero of this poem serves the god of wealth, Kubera, and having failed in some responsibility, has been cursed to live for a year in Rāmagiri in the Vindhyā mountains of Central India. The year proves too long to endure, for his lover—who remains unnamed—is a woman or yakṣī who lives in Alakā, a city in the distant Himālayas. The yakṣa is obsessed, he reminisces past moments with his lover and fantasizes that she too is lovesick for him. That said, *Meghadūtam* is much more than a fanciful love poem.

The yakṣa tries to motivate the cloud by describing the wonderful sights en route to Alakā, and the poem, thus, also works as a travelogue of an itinerary from the Vindhyās to the Himālayas. The route that the yakṣa recommends crosses specific mountains and rivers, and such towns as Vidiśā, Ujjayinī, Viśālā, Devagiri, Daśapura, Kurukṣetra, and so on, until we get to the romantic Alakā. This geography is resonant with cultural memory, and the route is presented as sacred, as a pilgrimage, and the locations are associated with gods and legends. There are references to the epics Mahābhārata and Rāmāyaṇa; Mt. Kailāsa in the Himālayas is the home of Śiva and Pārvatī; Alakā has palaces washed by moonlight from the crescent moon on Śiva's head; Devagiri is the residence of Skanda, Śiva's older son; and Ujjayinī has Mahākāla, the shrine to Śiva.

Kālidāsa shows us in Verse 5 that he is aware of the exaggerated concept of the poem and then continues to push the limits of the fancy, developing the personality of the cloud to its utmost; we are told of the cloud's illustrious lineage, history of exploits for the gods, and its receptivity to natural beauty. The landscape also responds to the cloud's aesthetic and erotic sensibilities, the earth yearns for its cooling showers, and women thrill at its touch. The yakṣa compares the cloud to Viṣṇu, to Śiva, and flatters it, appeals to its generosity, calls it friend, and even brother. At the end of the poem, we do not know if the cloud has said 'yes'.

The cloud's sky-location also becomes a point of view for the descriptions—remarkable if one recalls that Kālidāsa was writing at a time when there were no airplanes. The yakṣa describes the play of light on rivers and mountains, compares the texture of clayey river soil to dried mud-streaks on elephant skin, and even uses a perspective higher than the cloud's—the top angle of a cloud curled upon a mountain peak with slopes the hue of ripe-mango-laden trees is compared to a top view of a tuft of hair on a woman's breast of fair, tapering sides. *Meghadūtam* is written in the mandākrānta metre of seventeen-syllabic lines in a fixed order of long and short syllables, which has a slow and meandering rhythm. Each stanza is complete in itself, presenting one image or idea.

Over the centuries, *Meghadūtam* became a model for the genre of 'messenger-poem' with numerous imitations in Sanskrit and the vernacular.

1.

Some yakṣa who made a mistake was cursed by his master:
Suffer!
One entire year

An ordinary yakṣa
Not a hero

When even a season's separation is unbearable
Imagine six

What mistake
Kālidāsa does not specify
Some lapse of duty
Same word for 'duty' and 'right'

Has the hero lost the reader's heart
In the very first line?

Heavy the pangs of separation from his beloved

His prowess gone like a sun that's set
Year-long night

He lived in hermitages on a mountain
named after Rāma

Groves cool, waters pure
Sītā once bathed here

Remember Rāma remembered Sītā
Remember messenger Hanumān

Flying like a cloud

Why hermitages, in the plural?
More than exiled. Unsettled.

2.

Separated from her for months wasting on that mountain
The yakṣa looked lovesick

His gold bracelets had given his forearm the slip
Good lovers pine thin

Looked at a cloud embracing a ridge
on day one of the rainy season
like an elephant butting a rampart

Elephants sharpen tusks
on termite-hills or trees

The simile's a stretch
Kālidāsa knows
Wait two stanzas ...

And Kālidāsa calls the yakṣa's lover
'abalā': 'without-strength'

Just a generic word for a woman
in a stanza where a particular yakṣa
seems bereft of 'bala'

3.

In front of the cloud the stirrer of Ketaka flowers

The servant of the king of kings
The yakṣa, servant of the yakṣa-king
barely stood

Brooding
A long time
Tears pent

At the sight of a cloud even the mind of the contented
goes for a spin

Imagine a man whose beloved who longs to embrace him
lives far away

4.

Foreboding in the skies …

For the life of his love he wanted the giver of life, the cloud,
to carry news of his well-being

With a gift made of fresh Kuṭaja blossoms
and pleasing words—'welcome!'

5.

What! A cloud? A tumble of vapour, heat, water, wind

To deliver a message from sentient living beings

Not figuring that the eager yakṣa
asked it—him—cloud

The lovelorns' nature is such—poor things—
They cannot discriminate
between animate–inanimate

Kālidāsa calls him 'guḥyaka'
It means yakṣa, but also, 'mysterious'

Wearing his heart on his sleeve
Our yakṣa is anything but

6.

I know you—

You're born in the world-famous family of
Puṣkara and Āvartaka clouds

You're Indra's main aide
You take any shape you please

As for me
Far from family by a twist of fate
I've come to this state of imploring you

It's said
Plead to a superior even if in vain
Not to inferiors even if successful

7.

Raincloud, you're salve for those burning in love

You've got to take my message
Me—ripped by the wrath of wealth god Kubera

Take my message to Alakā, city of the yakṣa-king

Palaces washed by moonlight from the moon
on the head of Śiva situated, templed,
in the outer gardens

8.

Tossing curls
Sighing

Wives whose husbands are away will gaze at you
riding the wind-route

When you're here all ready
Who can ignore a pining wife?
No one

Unless—like me—slave to another

9.

Go without delay and you'll surely see
your brother's faithful wife alive

absorbed counting days

Women's hearts: like flowers
Prone to wilt in separation—

Hope's the tie that holds them up

For 'alive' our yakṣa says 'not-dead'
Hurry, cloud! She's in dire straits

10.

As a cool breeze nudges you slowly along
A proud Cātaka bird sings sweetly to your left

Your entourage in the sky a flock of cranes
in spectacular garland formation
to mate undercover

11.

Hearing that fortuitous sound the rumble
that makes earth a field of mushroom-umbrellas

Noble swans with lotus-stem-shreds in their beaks
Eager for Mānasarovar in the Himālayas

will fly along, your companions
all the way to Mt. Kailāsa

12.

Hug your dear friend, the high peak
Slopes marked with Rāma's footprints humans adore

Say bye

It's a friendship shaped by recurring meetings
and long separations' warm vapour exhalations

The mountain's resonant
with devotion and separation

13.

So listen as I tell you your journey's right route

Later, water-giver, you'll hear
my message with your eager ears

Placing your feet on peaks,
weary, ragged,

You'll sip some water from streams
and be on your way

14.

As naïve celestial women
Faces upturned
Alarmed:

'What! Does the wind blow the peak away?'

Up into the sky
Fly northwards

From these juicy cane fields

Steal away from the bossy, massive trunks of elephants
They guard eight directions

15.

Indra's bow *rainbow*
shines from the eastern hillock

A spectacle like shimmering gems
Your blue form's lit by it

Like Viṣṇu's figure *think blue*
in a cowherd guise *Kṛṣṇa*
Lit by a peacock plume

16.

The loving lovely eyes of country-women drink you
They think 'the crops depend on you'

They don't know the art of eyebrow-coquetry

Now climb a mound of fragrant ox-tilled earth

A short back-step *for momentum*
and go north again

17.

Mt. Mango-Peak hoists a travel-tired you
nicely on its head

You put out its forest fire with a strong shower once

Past favours in mind
Even the mean don't turn from friends in need

As for him who's this lofty
he'll host you, of course

18.

A must-see view for celestial lovers
in the sky:

You the colour of a glossy braid on mountaintop
Slopes glow with ripe forest-mangoes

Like earth's breast:
Dusky at the tip
Around it, fair

19.

A short stop in these woods
where foresters' wives pleasured

A faster gait from shed moisture
The next part's crossed

You'll see river Reva ragged
on rock-rugged Mt. Vindhyā's feet

Like holy-ash streaks etched on an elephant's limb

20.

Rain-spent, sip water from this current

Infused with bitter wild-elephant ichor
Slowed by rose-apple bushes

The wind does not shake you when laden, hey
Dense cloud, everyone's

Inconsequential when empty
Fullness, for gravitas

Elephants in heat exude ichor
It runs into streams where they bathe

Such sensuous liqueurs await
our thirsty cloud

21.

Forest antelopes

Spying green-brown Nīpa flowers with half-sprung stamens
And upcoming buds of Kandala along the banks
Sniffing overpowering earth fragrance in burned forests

Forest antelopes will mark
your dripping raindrops' path
A flight path traced on foot

22.

Celestials

Watching the Cātaka birds' clever catch
of celestial raindrops
A bird said to subsist on raindrops

Pointing out—enumerating—cranes in formation

Winning their dear bewildered wives' jittery embraces
at your rumble

The celestials will honour you
in gratitude

23.

For my darling's sake
For my happiness's sake

You'll want to go fast, but I imagine

You'll linger on this hill and that
Fragrant with Kakubha flowers

Welcomed by peacocks
with moist, white-edged eyes

I hope you'll get up, somehow,
and try to go quick

24.

At your arrival in the Ten Citadels
where geese have stayed a few days

A commotion

Shrub fringes a lighter shade
with new Ketaka flower spikes

In village squares
Birds starting to nest clamour
for leftover home-ritual offerings

Edges of the forest a ripe rose-apple purple

25.

Reaching Vidiśā the capital
famed in all directions
and named for that

Gain a sudden fulfilment of your lust

You'll suck the sweet water of river Vetravatī
Waves wavy like eyebrows knit on a face

A pleased rumble along her shore

26.

For a break, stay there in the hill called Nīca
with Kadamba flowers pert as if

erect at your touch

The hill advertizes

with grottoes that emit erotic aromas of prostitutes
The youthful exertions of city boys

27.

Relaxed, move on

with fresh raindrops sprinkling jasmine shrubs
in shore-gardens of forest streams

A moment's familiarity
Shading the faces of flower-gatherers

Wiping perspiring cheeks they bruise
the fading blue lotuses at their earlobes

28.

Ujjayinī's a detour for north-bound you

But don't turn your face from palace-roof displays
You're misled if you don't enjoy

Its city-women with darting eyes
scared of your lightning-wreath flashing

29.

When you meet Nirvindhyā on your way

Be full of amorous feeling

For a girdle she has a row of chirping birds
on her tossing waves

A lovely stagger serpentine

Navel's gyrations flaunted
Eddies

Women's first love expressions for a lover are thus
Flirtatious

30.

Hey Lucky!
Grieving your absence
Sindhu river proves your luck with her state

Old leaves fallen from trees on her banks

Pale waters braid

How will she stop wasting away?
You come up with a plan

31.

Reach Avanti
Village elders skilled in story-telling of King Udayana

Continue to Viśālā
Expansive city of expansive wealth

Like a luminous fragment of a divine realm come to earth

As if the remains of merit—dwindling merits—
of people of paradise, claimed

32.

Where at dawn the Śiprā breeze
Fragrant with the scent of burst-open blue lotuses

Prolongs the sharp, love-crazed cries of warbling cranes

Soothes limbs
Like a lover a flatterer who knows how to plead
eases the sexhaustion of women

33.

Ease your travel fatigue

Body bolstered by smoke let out by windows
from hair-scenting sessions

A dance—a gift—given by tame peacocks in fond amity

Watch the city's beauty in flower-fragrant palaces imprinted
with red lacquer from lovely women's feet

34.

As Śiva's attendants gaze at you, awed:
'Oh the colour of our Lord's throat'—Go

to the holy temple of the guru of three worlds
Śiva

Garden fanned by winds

Fragrant from fragrant water-lily pollens
of *fragrant river* Gandhavatī

Winds acrid from playful intent splashing bathing
young women

35.

And, water-bearer,

Reaching Śiva-shrine Mahākāla *cosmic time*
at the odd time of day, stay

When the sun's out of sight, beat
evening-ritual-temple-drums

A creditable thing to do for spear-holder Śiva

You'll reach your deep thunder's full pay-off

36.

Courtesans—

Girdles jangling to footwork

Hands weary with the slow waving
of gem-stemmed fans

Getting thrills of nail-scratches
at your early rain slashes

Unleashing sidelong glances at you
Honeybee row

37.

Then in the circle
When Śiva begins to dance

Lean on his high forest of arms

Decked in twilight new blood-red hibiscus flowers

Satiate his urge for bloody elephant hide

When Śiva killed elephant-demon Gajāsura
He wore its hide and danced in ecstasy

Your devotion spotted by Śiva's consort Bhavānī
Panic pacified, eyes at rest

38.

There on Ujjayinī roads in
impervious pin-piercing darkness

Women on the way to the homes of lovers

Lightning on touchstone
Show them the ground

Don't go clatter-shower-pitter-patter

They're timid

39.

Spent after lighting long hours

Your wife, Lightning, spent the night on some cornice
of sleeping pigeons

Sun seen, carry on with the rest of your journey

Those with promises to friends don't slack off

40.

Then quick! Out of the sun's way
He's back to take the dew from lotuses' faces
Husbands must hush tears from devastated wives' eyes

You interrupt his rays …
The offence won't be light

41.

Like a clear mind
River Gambhīrā waters

Even your shapely shadow's entry's easy

Then don't get cocky and snub
her darting winks—her frisky Śaphara fish

42.

Slipped from her curvaceous hips
to reed branches near

As if clutched by a hand
Her blue water-robe
You strip

Friend,
What a parting it will be for prone you

Who, who has known the pleasure
can give up a bared vulva?

43.

A cool breeze

Delectable from mix of earth scents your showers intensify
Slurp-sucked at elephant trunk tips
Wild fig ripening

A cool breeze will gently blow you
You want to go to Mt. Devagiri

44.

Skanda always lives there

Changing yourself into a floral cloud
Shower him
A flower-shower wet with sky-Gaṅgā waters

Skanda who?
New-moon wearer Śiva put his heat
Heat that outshines solar deity Āditya
in the mouth of the oblation-bearer god of fire, Agni
to save the armies of Indra

45.

Next, a roar that echoes in the mountains

Make fire-born Skanda's peacock dance
Sidelong glances lit by Śiva's moon

Motherly love makes Bhavānī set
a dropped plume of luminous orbs
at ears that usually get lotus petals

46.

Reed-born Skanda's honour done
Some distance past

Path clear of luted Siddha couples scared of raindrops

Bend low, mark Rantideva's fame, his sacrifice
of the daughters of Surabhi the mother of cows
reconfigured as low-flowing rivers on earth

Rantideva, the King of Daśapura
Sacrificed cows at rituals

Blood flowed rivers

Cambal the valley the river is also called
Carmaṇvatī forest-of-hides

47.

As you
Robber of the complexion of horn-bow archer
blue Viṣṇu
As you stoop to drink water

Sky-farers looking down see river Sindhu's broad current

Attenuated by distance to earth's pearl-string

A sapphire mass pendant in the centre

48.

River crossed, go
Your image playing to the curiosity of

Daśapura's women
Familiar with eyebrow-coquetry
Eyebrows creepers

Raised upper eyelashes gleam
A speckled effect steals the grace of bees
behind tossed Kunda flowers

49.

Now your shadow steps
on Brahmāvarta's pedestrian places

Note Kurukṣetra
Mahābhārata's battlefield
Scarred by the annihilation of Kurus

Where Gāṇḍīva bowman Arjuṇa
rained sharp arrows, hundreds,
on army chiefs' faces

Like how you pelt lotuses with torrents

50.

Going up to the waters of river Sarasvatī
Revered by plow-bearer Balarāma

Gentle Balarāma
War-averse from love for friends on both sides
Quit the coveted flavourful hala wine that
mirrored wife Revatī's eyes

Going up to Sarasvatī you too will be purified within
Dark only in complexion

51.

You must go then to Jahnu's daughter Gaṅgā
near Kanakhala

Rising from Mountain King Himālaya
Stairway for Sāgara's sons

Waves, hands, latched on to the moon
Tugged at Śiva's hair

She mocked the frown on Gauri's face
with her froth

When a penance calls on sky Gaṅgā's favour
She jumps
Śiva breaks her fall with his hair

Coiled in Śiva's hair, Gaṅgā
Neighbour to the moon
Daring co-wife to Gauri

52.

If you extend your front like a divine elephant

Think to drink aslant

Your shadow
on bright clear crystal winding current Gaṅgā

She would look very lovely, immediately
as if her confluence with river Yamunā
moved to another spot

Allāhabad—now called Prayāgrāj—
is where they mix
White Gaṅgā, blue Yamunā

53.

Arrive at Gaṅgā's birthplace

White snow-mountain

Rocks odorous with musk from the navels of resting deer

To clear the trip's fatigue, seated on its peak,
You'll look charming

As the dirt kicked up to the horn of the white bull
of three-eyed Śiva

Charming as dirt? Our yakṣa hides
A sense of humour

54.

In the blowing wind when a forest fire
from the friction of cedar stems singes
a single hair of a thick yak-tail

if it hurts the mountain
it's yours to douse
with a thousand jets of rain

Stopping the pain of those in trouble—
Payoff for the assets of the best

55.

All of a sudden there
Monsters called Śarabhas

In a flurry, keen
to pounce on you

Only to break their own limbs—

You've dodged the path

Scatter them with a clattering hailstorm

Are there any whose pointless sallies
do not end in ridicule?

56.

Evident on a rock there, footprints
of crescent-moon crested Śiva

Always adored by celestials with offerings

Sighting it, the faithful wish—
After the end of life, sins dusted off—
To be in Śiva's troop forever

57.

There, bamboo flutes filled with wind

Apsarās and their mates play melodious tunes
They sing of Śiva's victory of three cities

If your roar sounds like a drum in caves

That completes the orchestra
for Śiva

58.

At the foot of snow-mountain Himālaya
Past this and that sight
Go north

Swan-gate Curlew-pass
Gateway to the fame of Paraśurāma
who flung his axe, cleft the mountain

A nice oblique stretch like Viṣṇu's blue foot
raised to discipline Bali

Two steps covered the universe
Third step, on Bali's head

59.

Gone up to ridges cracked by the many arms
of ten-faced Rāvaṇa
when he tried to uproot the Himālaya
to replant in his garden

Be a guest of Kailāsa
High Himālaya
The mirror to divine women
who never grow old

Lotus-white peaks lifted and sprawled
There in the sky
Like three-eyed Śiva's laughter piling daily

60.

Up, I see you

Glossy crumbled eyeshadow
on fresh cut ivory-white mountain slope

like a blue garment on plough-bearer
Balarāma's shoulder

The mountain's beauty becomes
a sight to be stared at

61.

If Gauri traipses that playground-mountain by foot
with Śiva's stretched hand, snake-bracelet-free

You, arrived first
Devotion-bent
Figure re-arranged
Water-currents within withheld
You lay steps for her to climb the gem-slopes

62.

For sure there you bump into Indra's thunderbolt net
and burst out water

Young divine women think you a shower device

Friend,
Sweat-met, there's no escape

They're keen to play

Scare them with your roar, a macho sound

63.

Water-giver, arrive at that mountain
of clear crystals and changing light

Take water from the Mānasa lake
where golden lotuses grow

Put a pleasing fleeting veil
on Indra's elephant Airāvata's face

Wind-wash the muslin-like leaves
of the tree of desire

64.

Wanderer, not that you won't recognize Alakā city

Like a lover in high Himālaya's lap
Her robe, Gaṅgā, loose

At your arrival, she wears

Like a woman's hair 'alakā'
coiled in a net of pearls

Rain-shedding cloud-clusters in her towering heights

65.

Every feature is your equal in Alakā

Its lovely women	rival	your lightning
Its paintings		your rainbows
Its drums beaten to music		your deep vibrant sound
Its gem-studded floors		your water particles
Its cloud-licking turrets		your loftiness

66.

Lotuses dangling in the hands of wives

Hair plaited with Kunda flowers

Beauty of the face, fairer with Lodhra pollen dust

Fresh Kurabaka flowers around hair-braids

Śirīṣa flowers behind a pretty ear

Flower Nīpa shows up at the hair-parting when you arrive

67.

Where drunk bees buzz
Trees always in flower

Always a girdle of swans
on lakes with lotuses

Pet peacocks radiate plumes
necks stretched, calling, always

At dusk the moon always
bars the entrance to darkness

68.

Where tears arise for the wealthy for no other reason
than joy

No other suffering than Kāma's floral arrows
Resolved by union with the desired

No separation except by lovers' quarrels

No other age than youth

69.

White-gemmed palace terraces with star shaped
flower designs

Where yakṣas go with the best of women

To drink delicious passion-fruit of the
wish-fulfilling tree

At struck drum-skins, your deep sound

The wish-fulfilling tree
In Indra's garden
A pot of ambrosia under it

70.

Where young women *sought after by immortals*
play

Hiding gems in fistfuls of golden sand

Aired by winds cooled by Gaṅgā waters

Along riverbanks
Shaded from heat by Mandāra trees

71.

Where bold hands of lusty lovers toss robes
Slipped from loosened skirt-strings of red-lipped women—
Lips red as Bimba flowers

Shy, bewildered, the women throw
fists of dust at the tall flames of lamps

Though direct the aim
A wish in vain—
The lamps are gem-fired

72.

Where clouds that look like you

Led into top floors of buildings by
the ever-mobile guide wind

Smudge paintings with moisture

Then abruptly as if scared, they stumble
out of windows

in wisps imitating smoke vapours
They're cunning at that

73.

Where at midnight
By clear moonlight

Moonstones hung by threads on bed-frames release
the sexhaustion of limbs of women propped
on shoulders of embraced lovers

Moonstones absorb moisture from moonlight
Then exude it

74.

Where hedonists—endless money in their homes—with
sweet-voiced apsarās

Singing in high notes of the fame of
Kubera

Locked in conversation with madams, clever women

Daily enter the outer grove Vibhrāja

75.

Where at sunrise

Mandāra flowers dropped in a hurried gait
from braids

Broken scent-patches
Golden lotuses loosed from ears
Pearl-set hair nets
Garlands worn on breasts, strings snapped

These signs indicate the night-routes of lover-women

76.

Out of fear, thinking god Śiva, the friend of Kubera,
lives there in person in Alakā

Kāma does not usually carry
his bowstring made of bees

His venture's accomplished by the coquetries
of astute women

who bend eyebrows to simultaneously shoot
exact glances at targets of desire

Kāma's bow is sugarcane
Bowstring a line of bees
And each arrow tipped
with a different flower

77.

Where a wish-fulfilling tree produces

All ornaments for women
Garments galore
Honey to make eyes lively, suggestive
Flower sprigs with buds, alternatives to trinkets
And lacquer fit to lay on feet-lotuses

78.

There to the north of Kubera's house
Our family home

Identifiable from afar by a pretty gate
A king-of-gods' rainbow

Nearby a young Mandāra tree
Raised by my beloved like an adopted son

Weighed down by flower-clusters
within reach

79.

A pond too, here
Enclosed by emeralds
Emerald stepping stones

Thick with lotus blooms on glossy beryl stalks

Sorrows gone, swans have made its waters their home

Even when they see you, they do not remember
lake Mānasarovar nearby

80.

At its banks a mountain playground

Sapphires set in its peaks
Edged by golden plantain trees

It's dear to my wife
I remember it with a desperate mind

Specially, friend, when I see you flash
thunder at your edges
Blue peaks, gold edges

81.

Here, near the Mādhavī plant gazebo
fenced by Kurabaka bush

An Aśoka tree: red flowers, leaves flutter

And an adorable Kesara tree

The first hopes—as I do—to touch
your friend's left foot

The second, as if a craving pregnant woman craves
for the wine of her mouth

They say Kesara trees blossom
sprinkled with a mouthful of wine
And Aśoka trees when struck
by women's feet

82.

Between them

A crystal perch on a gold stand
Clamped with gems the colour of young bamboo

At the end of the day your friend, blue-throated peacock
rests here

A clap by my beloved,
A jangle of bangles
He's danced

83.

Keeping these signs in your heart, wise one,
Seeing

Pretty conch and lotus engravings on the threshold
You'll recognize the house

Of course, by my absence now
Dark and dismal

When the sun's away a lotus does not display
her graces

84.

Then morph into an elephant calf to land quickly

Settle on the nice peak of the mountain I told you about

You can go into the house
The view apparent by lightning

Glowing gently like a row of flickering fireflies

85.

The wife:

Slender
Dusky
Teeth jasmine buds

Ripe-Bimba-fruit lips
Startled-deer glances

Slim at the waist
Concave navel

A slow gait from heavy hips
A slight bow in the posture from heavy breasts

Among young women—who else
such an original creation of the creator

86.

Know her, my alter-ego
I, her companion, being far

Of moderate speech, alone like a Cakravāka bird

As heavy days of deep longing go by
The young girl will have changed, I think

Like a lotus shaken by winter

Cakravāka's a goose (or swan) that mates for life
Cursed to be parted from its mate

Found calling to each other from
opposite sides of a riverbank

87.

Beloved's eyes swollen *from crying*

Her lips discoloured from hot sighs

Cupped in her hand her face
Long hair shrouds her face partially

Like the moon, glory dimmed by your chase
Bearing the suffering

88.

Your sight will fall upon her
Praying, distraught

Or drawing a likeness of me imagined
Pining, emaciated

Maybe she asks the caged sweet-spoken Sārika bird
'Hey sensitive one, you were his favourite,

Do you recall my husband?'

89.

Gentle cloud,

Maybe she sits in shabby clothes
Lute in lap

About to sing in a high tone
A song with words marking my name

String wet with the tears of her eyes
Somehow tuned

Again and again she forgets the tune
though she composed it herself

90.

Flowers from the door
She places on the ground

Counts how many months remain (for reunion)
(how many days) since separation day

Or she savours our love kept in her heart

Such are the usual diversions of lovelorn women

91.

My absence does not bother your friend so much
in the daytime, busy

At night, with no recreation, I fear
the sorrow's heaviest

Soothe her with my message at midnight
Seated on the window of the house

Look—the loyal woman lies on the ground
sleepless

92.

On one side of the bed of separation, she lies

Grief thin like the moon's last sliver
on the eastern horizon

The night that went so soon with me
in lovemaking

The same night—long in separation
She passes in hot tears

93.

As her eyes go, for old time's sake,
towards the cool-nectar moonbeams entering
the window

They also withdraw, disturbed, heavy tears
covering lashes

Like a land lotus on a cloudy day
Neither close, nor open

94.

With hot sighs that dry her leaf lips

She tosses her hair, rough from plain-water baths
awry on her cheeks

She longs for sleep so somehow at least
in a dream, she might achieve

making love to me
But tears rob the chance

95.

At the end of the curse
When grief has gone

I must uncoil the braid she coiled
Forsaking flower wreaths

That very braid—tough, uneven
Rough to the touch

See her push from her cheeks out of discomfort
with unkempt nails

When husbands are away
Wives leave braids matted, neglected

96.

Ornaments off, that woman wears a delicate frame

Endlessly sad, her body falls again and again
in the lap of the bed

Full of fresh water, you'll rain tears, for sure

Those who are tender within
behave in compassionate ways

97.

I know your friend's, my wife's, heart is full of love for me

So I think of her in such a state in our first separation

A notion of being special has not made me boastful

Brother, all I've claimed will soon be evident to you

98.

Sidelong glances blocked by loose strands of hair

Missing sheen of eyeliner

Refraining from wine, forgot how to arch eyebrows

I think the doe-eyed woman's upper eyelid trembles
at your approach

Lovely like a lily in a flutter
from the current of fish

99.

Her left thigh …

Habituated to a massage by my hands after lovemaking

Fair like the stem of a juicy plantain tree

My nail marks faded

The familiar pearl-net stocking discarded
in her ill-fated state

The twitch of her left thigh …

100.

Rain-giver, just then,
if she has found the comfort of sleep

Seated near her, hold your thunder, wait
through the second watch of the night

May the tight embrace
of her vine-arms around my neck

That have somehow found me, her lover,
In a dream, not drop abruptly

A night has three parts called watches

101.

Awakened with a breeze cooled by your own spray

As good as renewed by clusters of Mālatī flowers

When she looks at your seat with steady eyes

Lightning held back in your belly
In earnest speech rumble
To the honourable lady,
Start to speak:

102.

'Unwidowed woman,

Know me your husband's dear friend
who has come to you

A water-carrier, carrying his news in the heart

With a deep, smooth rumble, I am he
who hurries herds of tired travellers

on the way home, eager
to uncoil their women's braids'

103.

When this has been said

She, face raised
Like Sītā to Hanumān, the wind-god's son
Recall verse one

Seeing you and taking you in

Heart heaving
She will hear all that follows with rapt intent

Gentle cloud,
News of the beloved brought by a friend

Comes close to a meeting for married women

104.

Long-living cloud,

Do yourself proud from my message
Tell her this:

'Woman, your companion stays without danger
in the hermitage of Rāmagiri

Separated from you, he asks how you are'

For living beings prone to problems
This is the first address

105.

'The far-off yakṣa, his way blocked by hostile fate

By the force of imagination, enters your state

With his thinner body, your thin body
With his deep suffering, your suffering
With his fast tears, your unstoppable tears
With his heaving, your heaving
With sighs hotter than your sighs

106.

'He who was keen to whisper in your ears

that which can be said before your friends
from the desire to touch your face, yes,

He, beyond your earshot, beyond your sight

He said through my mouth, these
words composed with longing

107.

'I see your limb in the Śyāma vine

The way your look falls in the glance of the startled doe

The mellow glow of your face in the moon

Your hair in lush peacock-feathers

The arching of your brows in the river's little waves

But alas! Oh Disaster! There's
no equal to you in any one thing

108.

'After painting you on a rock with red pigment
Painting you feigning anger

When I want to draw myself falling at your feet

My sight blurs, tearful again then

Cruel fate, cannot tolerate our union even there
Even on the painting

109.

‘When my arms stretch into the sky to hold you
in a tight cruel embrace, somehow found
in a dream vision

Are those teardrops large as pearls
that fall on leaves of trees probably
not of earth-spirits watching?

110.

‘Fragrant with the flowing sap of just-burst tight leaf-buds
of Deodar trees

Those snow-mountain winds blow south

Good woman,

They’re embraced by me, thinking
they may have first touched your body, yes?

111.

‘How can the long night of three watches be
Shortened to a moment

How can the day have gentle warmth
in all seasons

Woman with darting eyes,
Such are the impossible wishes of my mind

Left with no other recourse by the deep
intense suffering of your separation

112.

'Speculating a lot, I depend on myself

You too, good woman, must not be discouraged

Whose lot is endless happiness
Or only misery?

Circumstance—like the path of a wheel-rim
Goes down, and up

113.

'When Viṣṇu rises from his snake-bed,
The end of my curse

Close your eyes
Pass the remaining four months

On full-moon lit autumn nights we will enjoy
our heart's desires that separation intensified

Viṣṇu sleeps through four months of rains
in the second part of the year

114.

'And he said,

Long ago in bed, although necking, you
fell asleep

Crying aloud for some reason
Woke up with a jolt

Again and again when I asked, you said,
laughing to yourself

"You rogue,
I saw you in my dream
Enjoying someone else"

115.

'From such confidences, learn that I am well

Dark-eyed, don't become distrustful of me
from rumours

It's said affections wear off a little by separation
But really, lack of pleasure intensifies

taste for objects of desire
Affections become a mass of love'

116.

Thus consoling your friend
In the extreme grief of first separation

With those words of my remembrance and well-being
Sustain my life, fragile as morning Kunda flowers

Descend from the hill
Peaks chipped by the horns
of the bull of the three-eyed Śiva

Kunda blooms in the evening

117.

Gentle cloud, is this on?
This friendly favour

to me
by you?

I do not assume your seriousness
as refusal

Silently even, you give water
to the beseeching Cātaka birds
that subsist on raindrops

Good people respond only by doing
what their dear ones want

118.

Whether from friendship
Or a compassionate bent, thinking me
miserable

Do this good turn for me
Me who made an inappropriate wish

Then, water-giver, travel to the places you want
Your grace increased by rain

May there be no separation
Even for a moment

Between you and your lightning

ABHIJÑĀNA ŚĀKUNTALAM

Śakuntalā's Souvenir

The most well-known Sanskrit play from India, *Abhijñāna Śākuntalam* is the story of the romance, separation and reunion of King Duṣyanta and Śakuntalā, the daughter of an apsarā (celestial nymph) and a sage. The plot begins with Duṣyanta hunting in a forest, inadvertently too close to the peaceful hermitage of Sage Kaṇva. The sage is away, and the king is welcomed by his foster daughter Śakuntalā and her friends Priyaṃvadā and Anasūyā. Duṣyanta and Śakuntalā fall in love at first sight, and marry in private according to the Gāndharva style, which requires no witnesses or rituals. When recalled to his duties, Duṣyanta leaves, giving Śakuntalā his royal signet ring as a token and promising to send for her. A few days after their separation, Śakuntalā is visited by the sage Durvāsa, known for his egoism and short temper. When she—daydreaming and distracted—does not greet him appropriately, Sage Durvāsa is infuriated. The angry sage curses her that the object of her reverie will not remember her. Cajoled by Śakuntalā's friends, the sage relents and offers her a reprieve: The king's memory will return only if he sees the token ring. Sage Kaṇva returns, and a pregnant Śakuntalā is duly escorted to Duṣyanta's palace. When Duṣyanta does not recognize her, Śakuntalā looks for the ring to trigger his memory and finds it missing. Duṣyanta cannot be persuaded to remember who she is, nor their meeting and marriage, and a humiliated Śakuntalā is rescued—taken away by her celestial mother. Sometime later, a fisherman finds the ring (which was swallowed by a fish in a river where Śakuntalā had dipped her hand), tries to sell it, and is caught by the king's guards. Duṣyanta's memory returns the moment he lays eyes on the ring and he is plunged into deep remorse. Invited by Indra to help the gods in a war, Duṣyanta travels to the celestial world, and to the hermitage of Marīci (son of the creator, Brahma), where he fortuitously runs into his son by Śakuntalā—Bharata. The parents are reunited.

If Duṣyanta's paeans are sometimes cloying and his remorse melodramatic, they are tempered by the realism in his conversations with the court jester. The jester's cynical observations and witty repartee downplay the king's romantic excesses. Moreover, the moment one looks beyond the theme of erotic love, they find an entire range of emotions in the play. Memorable moments include Sage Kaṇva's sense of lightness when his daughter leaves for her husband's home, when the ascetic accuses the king of pawing Śakuntalā, when Sarvadamana insists on having his way, and when Śakuntalā declines the ring in the last act. Indian criticism has particularly appreciated the moments of separation in the fourth act—between Śakuntalā and the deer, between Kaṇva and Śakuntalā, and between Śakuntalā and her friends.

The story of Duṣyanta and Śakuntalā is also present in the Mahābhārata. If Kālidāsa borrowed from it, he also made considerable changes. The Śakuntalā of the Mahābhārata is pragmatic and feisty—before consenting to marry the king, she negotiates that her son will be heir. When rejected by the king, she is outraged and argues for her rights. And Duṣyanta is simply a cad in the Mahābhārata story—no curse, no memory lapse—just trying to get away with betrayal. In Kālidāsa's plot, the intervention of the curse justifies Duṣyanta's actions. Additionally, Kālidāsa fashions an ideal man and king in Duṣyanta. Kālidāsa's Duṣyanta is so integrated, his passions so well aligned with his understanding of morality, he cannot act or even *think* inappropriately—for example, his very attraction to Śakuntalā must mean she cannot be an ascetic woman. When Śakuntalā arrives at his court, he hesitates even to look at her because he will not look at (whom he thinks as) another man's wife.

In the eighteenth century, as East India Company officers sought to gain an insight into the Indian way of thinking, the play was hailed as a window into Indian culture. Sir William Jones translated it into Latin, and then into English, and saw in it a glorious past of Indian civilization, with kings and heroes. He explained Marīci as a signifier of light and Kaśyapa as a personification of infinite space. His translation also toned down the sexuality of the play, glossing over some of Kālidāsa's expressions appreciating Śakuntalā's physical beauty. Jones's assessment also saw the entire jester section as redundant. For European romantics, Kālidāsa's play only expressed a pristine (and primitive) connection to nature, an idyllic world of hermitages in forests inhabited by dreamy mystics and virgins playing with antelopes. Jones's translation was praised as a literary work to match ancient Greek plays. Wolfgang von Goethe was so struck by it, he said it 'charmed and enraptured' the soul. Some of this romanticism was replaced by a more critical view later on in the colonial era, as with a translation by Monier-Williams; yet, the nation-making Indians saw Indian spirituality in this play. Rabindranath Tagore's essay on the play's inner meaning speaks of the spiritual simplicity of Śakuntalā, and discusses how the curse and separation help sublimate the gross sexuality of the lovers into their spiritual union. Romila Thapar reads the story of Śakuntalā as a lens into history, and shows how different versions and responses to the play illumine historical moments.

Kālidāsa's changes to the storyline may show how attitudes to women changed since the version in the Mahābhārata. Interpretations over the last few centuries also reveal to us the changing perspectives and ideals of those reading the play. In contemporary criticism and anthologies of world literature, what gets emphasized is its literary craft—attention is drawn to how Kālidāsa establishes Śakuntalā's kinship to nature, or how moments within the play work together to build an amplified drama of such broader philosophical problems as memory and forgetting.

CAST OF CHARACTERS

DUṢYANTA: The king

ŚAKUNTALĀ: Duṣyanta's lover; daughter of Menakā; foster daughter of Kaṇva

ANASŪYĀ AND PRIYAṂVADĀ: Śakuntalā's friends

GAUTAMĪ: Female ascetic

MĀDHAVYA: The court jester; Duṣyanta's childhood friend

MENAKĀ: A celestial artiste renown for her beauty ('apsarā'), and Śakuntalā's mother

KAṆVA: A sage; Śakuntalā's foster father

SĀNUMATĪ: Menakā's friend

SARVADAMANA: Śakuntalā and Duṣyanta's son

MĀTALI: Indra's messenger and charioteer

RAIVATAKA: Duṣyanta's guard

KARABHAKA: Duṣyanta's mother's messenger

KAÑCUKĪ: Duṣyanta's chamberlain

YAVANI: Duṣyanta's attendant

VETRAVATĪ AND PRATIHĀRĪ: Female door-guards of King Duṣyanta

ŚĀRṄGARAVA, ŚĀRADVATA, VAIKHĀNASA, GAUTAMA, HĀRĪTA: Kaṇva's disciples

GĀLAVA: Kaśyapa's disciple

BHADRASENA: Army-chief

CATURIKĀ, PARABHṚTIKĀ AND MADHUKARIKĀ: Duṣyanta's maidservants

SUVRATĀ: Sarvadamana's nanny

KAŚYAPA: Sage; son of sage Marīci

ADITI: Kaśyapa's consort

FISHERMAN: The one who spots the souvenir ring inside a fish's belly

POLICE OFFICER: Duṣyanta's brother-in-law

SŪCAKA AND JĀNUKA: Two policemen

HAMSAPĀDIKĀ: Duṣyanta's ex-lover

VASUMATĪ: Duṣyanta's queen

DHANAMITRA: A merchant

TWO BARDS

OTHER CHARACTERS MENTIONED:

KAUŚIKA: Śakuntalā's real father

DURVĀSA: A sage known for egotism and bad temper

NĀRADA: A sage

INDRA: Chief of the gods

JAYANTA: Indra's son

ACT I

(*Benediction*)

May Śiva …

Here, visible

Embodied, accessible

In eight forms, perceptible:

> WATER creator's first creation
> FIRE carries ritual offerings
> PRIEST vedic
> SUN-MOON timekeepers two
> SPACE fixed, permeates the universe, its sound heard
> EARTH called womb of all seeds
> AIR how living beings have life

May Śiva protect you

(*After the benediction*)

PRESENTER: (*Looks at the wings*) If the backstage routine is over, do come here.

ACTRESS: (*Enters*) I'm here.

PRESENTER: This audience is mostly the intelligentsia. We've got to entertain them today with a new play called *Abhijñāna Śākuntalam,* composed by Kālidāsa. Your task, then, is to be mindful of every character.

ACTRESS: With your good direction, nothing will go wrong.

PRESENTER: I'll tell you a fact of life.

> I think my stagecraft is no good
> until the critics are happy

Even trained geniuses
lack self-confidence

ACTRESS: That's true. Tell me what to do next.

PRESENTER: What else? Treat the ears of the audience! Then sing about this delightful summer that has begun.

Summer days …

Happy bathing in *waaaters*

Jungle-breezes perfumed by
pāṭala *flowwers*

Dozing's easy in the *shaaade*

The evenings especially *goood*

ACTRESS: Okay.

Ardent women wear earrings
of Śirīṣa blossoms *tennderly* while

Lightly-lightly the bees kiss
oh-so-delicate filament tips

PRESENTER: Well sung! The audience all around is like a still-life painting, stunned by your melody. What play shall we entertain them with now?

ACTRESS: Didn't the audience request, right at the outset, that we stage a new play called *Abhijñāna Śākuntalam*?

PRESENTER: Good reminder, I forgot that just then.

I was carried away by your
song's alluring melody

Like this King Duṣyanta
by the wind-speedy antelope

(*Exit*)

(*End of Prologue*)

(*Enter: By chariot, chasing a deer, the charioteer and King Duṣyanta armed with a bow and arrow*)

CHARIOTEER: (*Looks at the king and at the deer*)

As I eye
the black-spotted deer
and your strung bow, it's

As if I see
bow-bearer Śiva himself
chasing a deer

DUṢYANTA: Charioteer, we've been enticed very far by this deer. But even now, he …

From time to time
a graceful neck-stretch

to direct a look
at the fast chariot,

Haunches hunched
into chest

from fear
of the arrow's fall,

Half-chewed Darbha-
-grass strewn path

spilling from tired
sagging jaws,

Look how
by leaps and bounds

Hardly on the ground
He mostly flies

(*With surprise*) How closely I chase him, and yet he's so hard to spot.

CHARIOTEER: King, the chariot's speed has slowed down because I drew in the reins, for I thought the ground uneven. That's how the deer could put this distance between us. Now that we're on even ground, it won't be difficult to get him.

DUṢYANTA: Then slacken the reins.

CHARIOTEER: As the king says. (*Mimes the momentum of the chariot*) King, look, see—

Now that the reins are loose …

Stretched fore
The horses run

As if intolerant
of the speedy deer

Ears erect stiff
Plume-tips motionless

Can't be overtaken
even by the dust

they flung up
themselves

DUṢYANTA: True. The horses run faster than Indra's fawn-coloured horses. So:

Thanks to the chariot's speed …

What's usually puny
suddenly stands out

What's cut in the middle
is apparently joined

Eyes find straight what's
naturally crooked

Nothing's far nor near
even for a second

Charioteer, see it being killed. (*Fixes arrow to bow*)

VOICE BACKSTAGE: King! Don't kill, don't kill, this is a deer of the āśrama.

CHARIOTEER: (*Listens and looks*) Hermits stand between your arrow's trajectory and the deer.

DUṢYANTA: Then let the horses be reined in.

CHARIOTEER: As you wish. (*Stops the chariot*)

(*Vaikhānasa, a hermit, enters with another hermit*)

VAIKHĀNASA: (*Raises hand*) Hey King, don't kill, this is a deer of the āśrama.

No no no arrow fall

on this delicate deer body
Like fire on a heap of flowers

What a deer life
Too fragile

How piercing the cascade
of your adamantine arrows

Withdraw that well-fastened arrow
about to blast

Your weapon's meant
to protect the distressed

Not to hurl
at the blameless

DUṢYANTA: I take it back. (*Does as he says*)

VAIKHĀNASA: This is worthy of you, light of the Puru race.

It's appropriate of you
born in the Puru race

May you have a son-emperor
with the same grace

BOTH HERMITS: (*Raise hands*) May you have an emperor-son!

DUṢYANTA: (*With folded hands*) The brahmin's word is accepted.

VAIKHĀNASA: King, we are on our way to collect kindling. Here, on the banks of Anumālinī, the āśrama of Sage Kaṇva may be seen. If it doesn't get in the way of other business, go in and accept their hospitality. Moreover:

When you see how
the daily rituals of ascetics
are freed of dangers

You'll know how well your
bowstring-scarred shoulder
protects them

DUṢYANTA: Is the patriarch Kaṇva there?

VAIKHĀNASA: Only recently, putting his daughter Śakuntalā in charge of hospitality, he went to Somatīṛtha to appease her unfavourable destiny.

DUṢYANTA: Fine, I'll see her. She'll surely tell the great sage about my evident respect for him.

VAIKHĀNASA: We'll carry on then. (*Exits with disciple*)

DUṢYANTA: Prod the horses. Let's purify ourselves with a sight of the hermitage.

CHARIOTEER: Whatever the king commands. (*Again, mimes the speed of the chariot*)

DUṢYANTA: (*Looks all around*) Even without being told, it is obvious we are at the border of the āśrama.

CHARIOTEER: How so?

DUṢYANTA:

Beneath trees
wild rice grains fallen
from mouths of parrots in hollows

Here and there
oily stones suggest
crushed Iṅgudi fruits

Grown confident
unruffled deer endure
unfamiliar noise

Lake paths streaked
by dripping edges
of bark garments

CHARIOTEER: All that's true.

DUṢYANTA: (*Goes a little further*) And also—

Tree roots washed by water run-offs
channelled by fast winds
Thus, kitchens

Bright leaf-buds paled by smoke
rising from butter offerings
So, fire altars

Fearless fawns graze slowly here
in meadows of cut Darbha-grass shoots
Then, cut for ritual use

DUṢYANTA: Charioteer, let's not be a disturbance to the āśrama residents. Stop the chariot right here so I can get down.

CHARIOTEER: I've held the reins. Fine to get off, King.

DUṢYANTA: (*Gets off*) Charioteer, āśramas must be entered in modest clothes. Take this then. (*Takes off jewellery and bow, gives them to the charioteer*) Make sure that the horses are watered by the time I get back from visiting the residents of the hermitage.

CHARIOTEER: Okay. (*Exits*)

DUṢYANTA: (*Walks and observes*) Here's the gate to the āśrama. I'll go in right away. (*Enters; senses a good energy*)

Peace the mark of this āśrama
Yet my arm throbs

The result of what? Or

Why do doors show up everywhere
when something's destined

VOICE BACKSTAGE: This way, this way, friends.

DUṢYANTA: (*Listens*) Uh, I hear conversation from the south of the orchard. I'll go there now. (*Walks and observes*) Some hermit-girls, coming just this way to water plants, with pitchers in sizes that match their own figures. (*Observes closely*) The sight of these girls … delightful!

> This loveliness of āśrama people
> can't be found in palaces
>
> Forest vines by far surpass
> the beauty of garden-creepers

I'll wait in this shade and watch. (*Stays there, looks*)

(*Enter: Śakuntalā with friends, acting as described*)

ŚAKUNTALĀ: This way, this way, girls.

ANASŪYĀ: Dear Śakuntalā, I guess that the trees of the āśrama are more dear than you to father Kaṇva, for you've been selected to fill these basins at the foot of trees, although you're as delicate as the Navamallikā flower.

ŚAKUNTALĀ: It's not just my father's order. I have a sisterly affection for them too. (*Waters plants*)

DUṢYANTA: What! Is this Kaṇva's daughter? In this instance, it doesn't seem right that the sage—senior as he may be—puts her to āśrama-errands.

> The sage who wants
> to make this innocent charm
> capable of penance
>
> Tries to cut a Śamī-plant stem
> with the edge of a blue
> lotus petal

Let it be. I'll hide behind this tree, so I can look at her freely.

ŚAKUNTALĀ: Dear Anasūyā, I feel restrained by this bark cloth that Priyaṃvadā fastened so tightly. Please loosen it.

ANASŪYĀ: Yes. (*Loosens it*)

PRIYAṂVADĀ: (*With a laugh*) Why accuse me! Blame your own youthfulness that causes your breasts to swell!

DUṢYANTA: Well said.

> Full pair of breasts concealed by bark
> Tied in a tight knot at the shoulder
>
> Like a flower wrapped in pale sepal
> Her fresh beauty doesn't reveal its grace

Of course the bark is unsuited to her beauty. On the other hand, doesn't it enhance her beauty like an ornament?

> Though surrounded by weeds
> the lotus is charming
>
> Though murky, the moon's
> blemish displays grace
>
> Even in a bark dress
> this girl's very lovely
>
> For delightful figures
> What isn't an ornament?

ŚAKUNTALĀ: (*Looks ahead*) These fluttering buds, fingers, of the Kesara plant … as if they call on me to hurry. I'll go over to it then.

PRIYAṂVADĀ: Śakuntalā, hold on there for a second.

ŚAKUNTALĀ: Why?

PRIYAṂVADĀ: With you beside it, the Kesara plant seems mated with a creeper.

ŚAKUNTALĀ: No wonder you're called 'Priyaṃvadā', the 'sweet-talker'.

DUṢYANTA: What Priyaṃvadā said to Śakuntalā is not just sweet, but true.

> Lower lip, tender-leaf hue
>
> Arms, delicate vines twining
>
> Youthfulness loaded in her limbs
> Covetable as a blossom

ANASŪYĀ: Śakuntalā, that Navamallikā creeper, self-appointed bride of the mango tree, is the one you named 'Vanajyotsnā'—'forest moonlight'—have you forgotten?

ŚAKUNTALĀ: Then I'll forget myself. The mutual love of this creeper and tree happened in a pleasant season! Vanajyotsnā—young, with new blossoms. The mango tree full of fruit, ready to enjoy her.

PRIYAṂVADĀ: Anasūyā, do you know why Śakuntalā stares so much at Vanajyotsnā?

ANASŪYĀ: I have no idea, do tell.

PRIYAṂVADĀ: She thinks—'Just as Vanajyotsnā has got together with a suitable tree, may I also get a suitable mate.'

ŚAKUNTALĀ: Oh really, I think, this is a wish you have for yourself. (*Empties the watering jar*)

DUṢYANTA: Could she be born to the patriarch by a woman who isn't of his own kind? Be done with doubts …

> No doubt she's fit for a kṣatriya to marry
> For my noble heart desires her

When righteous people are in uncertain situations
Intuition's the jury

And yet, I'll find out the truth about her

ŚAKUNTALĀ: (*Flustered*) Oh my! A bee's heading towards my face, roused from the jasmine by the commotion of sprinkling water. (*Mimes being bothered by the bee*)

DUṢYANTA: (*Looks longingly*)

Probing her identity, I'm lost

but you, bee, you're blessed,
you almost touch her darting, tremulous eye

Roving around her ear you buzz softly
like someone murmuring secrets

Even as her hands flail, you sip
her lip the sum of pleasure

ŚAKUNTALĀ: This rascal doesn't stop. I'll go elsewhere. (*Stands in a different place and looks around*) How come, it comes here too! Girls, save me from being assaulted by this rude bee.

ANASŪYĀ AND PRIYAMVADĀ: (*Smile*) Who are we to save you? Call out to Duṣyanta. The āśrama is supposed to be protected by the king.

DUṢYANTA: It's necessary to show myself. Take it easy, take it easy. (*Speaking to himself, pauses*) But this way, my position as the king will be found out. Okay. I'll speak like this…

ŚAKUNTALĀ: (*Steps aside, and casts a glance*) What? It follows me here too!

DUṢYANTA: (*Goes forward quickly*)

> When Paurava,
> The punisher of the wicked
> rules the earth
>
> Who misbehaves like this
> with innocent hermit-girls?

(*Looking at the king, everyone's confused*)

ANASŪYĀ: Sir, it's not that important. (*Points to Śakuntalā*) Our friend here, troubled by a bee, got scared.

DUṢYANTA: (*Faces Śakuntalā*) Does your meditation go well?

(*Confused, Śakuntalā remains speechless*)

ANASŪYĀ: All's well, thanks to a special guest. Śakuntalā dear, go to the āśrama. Bring fruits and other things. This water will be for washing his feet.

DUṢYANTA: Your courteous words complete the hospitality.

PRIYAMṾADĀ: Even so, Sir, do sit for a moment on this platform under the cool shade of this Saptaparṇa tree, ease your weariness.

DUṢYANTA: For sure you too must be tired by this work. Sit down for a moment.

ANASŪYĀ: Śakuntalā, it's appropriate for us to look after guests. Let's sit here.

ŚAKUNTALĀ: (*To herself*) Wonder why, seeing this person, I'm lost in an emotion that's incompatible with an āśrama.

DUṢYANTA: (*Looks at all of them*) The friendship between all of you is all the more charming because you're all of the same age, and look.

PRIYAṂVADĀ: (*Aside*) Anasūyā, who could this be … Looks sharp and dignified, talks in a sweet and pleasant manner … he seems powerful.

ANASŪYĀ: My friend, the same curiosity gets me too! I'll just ask. (*Aloud*) The confidence produced by Sir's nice conversation prompts me … What noble-royal family does Sir enhance?—What's the land, whose people now mourn your absence—What has put you, so delicate, to the trouble of coming to an āśrama?

ŚAKUNTALĀ: (*To herself*) Heart, don't fret, Anasūyā asks exactly what you wondered about.

DUṢYANTA: (*To himself*) What now? Disclose myself, or conceal myself? All right, I'll put it this way. (*Aloud*) Ma'am, I'm the one appointed by the king of the Puru race to protect dharma. I've come to this holy forest to check if the vedic rituals are trouble-free.

ANASŪYĀ: Then the followers of dharma now have a protector.

(*Śakuntalā mimes lovestruck shyness*)

ANASŪYĀ AND PRIYAṂVADĀ: (*Noting among themselves the king and Śakuntalā's state*) Oh Śakuntalā, if only father Kaṇva were here today.

ŚAKUNTALĀ: (*Peeved*) What then?

ANASŪYĀ AND PRIYAṂVADĀ: He'll make this special guest gratified by giving him his life's treasure.

ŚAKUNTALĀ: Go away, you two. You speak with some wild notion in your heads. I won't listen to your words.

DUṢYANTA: Then I too have a question for you both about your friend.

ANASŪYĀ AND PRIYAṂVADĀ: Sir, your request is like a favour.

DUṢYANTA: Holy Kaṇva has always been celibate. How can your friend here be his daughter?

ANASŪYĀ: Then know about our friend. There is a master sage of great power with the family name of Kauśika.

DUṢYANTA: Yes, I've heard.

ANASŪYĀ: Know him to be our friend's real father. By raising her and so on, Sage Kaṇva is now the abandoned Śakuntalā's father.

DUṢYANTA: My curiosity's aroused by the word 'abandoned'. I'd like to hear her story from the beginning.

ANASŪYĀ: Listen, Sir. Long ago, on the bank of river Gautamī, an apsarā called Menakā broke the self-control of the meditating master-sage on the bank. She was sent by the gods—who, for some reason, were afraid…

DUṢYANTA: There's fear in the gods about others' penance! What next!

ANASŪYĀ: Then, at the start of spring, looking at Menakā's intoxicating form … (*Pauses halfway from shyness*)

DUṢYANTA: I understand what followed. So she was born of an apsarā.

ANASŪYĀ: Right.

DUṢYANTA: It's apt.

> How's such beauty's birth possible in mortals
> Dazzling lightning doesn't rise from the earth

(*Śakuntalā continues to look coy*)

DUṢYANTA: (*To himself*) My desires have found the opportunity. Hearing the jokingly declared wish by her friend, for a husband for Śakuntalā, my heart's disturbed with divided feelings.

PRIYAṂVADĀ: (*Observing Śakuntalā with a smile and turning towards the hero*) Sir, you look like you want to say something again…

(*Śakuntalā raises a forefinger as if to stop her*)

DUṢYANTA: Ma'am, you have it well figured. Out of eagerness to hear about people of good conduct, I have something else to ask.

PRIYAṂVADĀ: Enough of this hesitation; hermits can be questioned without reservation.

DUṢYANTA: (*To himself*) This is what I want to ask:

> Is the ascetic vow that
> stops Kāma's dealings only
> to be followed until she's wed?
>
> Or oh! Will she live forever
> with the deer darlings who
> have eyes like hers?

PRIYAṂVADĀ: Sir, in following dhārmic duties, she is under others' control. But her father's wish is to give her to a suitable husband.

DUṢYANTA: (*To himself*) The wish is not hard to realize.

> Heart, stay hopeful, now
> There's an answer to the doubt
>
> What you suspected was fire
> Is a jewel that can be touched.

ŚAKUNTALĀ: (*Annoyed*) Anasūyā, I will leave now!

ANASŪYĀ: Reason?

ŚAKUNTALĀ: I'll complain to Gautamī Madam about this Priyaṃvadā who is busy talking nonsense.

ANASŪYĀ: Śakuntalā, it's not appropriate, your going away as you fancy, leaving unfinished the hospitality due a distinguished guest.

(*Śakuntalā starts to leave without saying anything*)

DUṢYANTA: (*Wanting to reach her, restraining himself. Says to himself*) Lovers' desires are reflected in actions. Indeed, I …

Going after the ascetic's daughter—the nerve
Abruptly checked by propriety

It's as if having gone, I returned already
Though I did not budge from my place

PRIYAMVADĀ: (*Stops Śakuntalā*) Hey, it's not okay for you to leave!

ŚAKUNTALĀ: (*Knits her brows*) Why?

PRIYAMVADĀ: You owe me two tree-waterings. Come on now, free yourself of this debt and then you can leave.

DUṢYANTA: Ma'am, I see that she is, in fact, tired from watering trees. For:

Lifting the water-pitcher …

Drooping shoulders, palms very ruddy
Panting makes her breasts heave, even now
The Śirīṣa ear-flower stuck to the sweat-net on her face
Hair-braid undone, hair awry, held back by a hand

I'll set her free from what she owes… (*Wants to give his ring*)

(*Both look at each other after reading the name on it*)

DUṢYANTA: Don't get strange ideas about me. This is a king's gift. Be aware, I am a kingly person.

PRIYAMVADĀ: Surely then it's not right for this ring to be separated from your finger. By Sir's words, she's free from debt now. (*Slight smile*) Hey Śakuntalā, you've been freed by this compassionate gentleman, or by the great king. Go now.

ŚAKUNTALĀ: (*To herself*) If only I were my own mistress! (*Aloud*) Who are you to stop me, or set me free? How come?

DUṢYANTA: (*Looks at Śakuntalā, says to himself*) Is it possible she is towards me, as I am towards her? Why then, my desire's fulfilled.

Although she does not mix
her speech with my words,

She lends her ears
as I speak

For sure she doesn't stand
facing my face

but mostly her eyes
have no other aim

VOICE BACKSTAGE: Ascetics! Be ready to protect the animals of the hermitage. King Duṣyanta, who enjoys hunting, is nearby.

Horse-hoof-struck dust falls
thick like a locust swarm
the colour of late twilight
on wet-bark garments
hung on the āśrama trees

And

An elephant enters
the holy forest

Like an incarnate
obstacle to penance

Scared by the sight
of a chariot

Struck by a sharp cut
A stem stuck to a tusk
A tangled net of vines
dragged by his foot

Flock of deer, scattered

(*Everyone, hearing, somewhat confused*)

DUṢYANTA: Oh no. Soldiers in search of me disturb the forest. All right. I'll go back then.

ANASŪYĀ: We're upset by this news about the forest. Allow us to go back to the hermitage.

DUṢYANTA: (*With agitation*) Ladies, go. We too will make an effort so that there will be no disturbance to the āśrama.

(*Everyone gets up*)

ANASŪYĀ AND PRIYAṂVADĀ: Sir, our hospitality could not be completed. Embarrassed, we ask to see you again.

ŚAKUNTALĀ: Anasūyā, my foot's hurt by a shoot of Kuśa grass. My bark garment is stuck to a Kurabaka branch. Wait for me while I free myself.

DUṢYANTA: I feel disinterested to go back to town. I'll join my group and set up camp not too far from the āśrama. I'm unable to distract myself from thinking about Śakuntalā.

My body moves forward—
Mind stays back

Like the china-silk of a flag
on a chariot
in leeward wind

(*Everyone exits*)

END OF ACT I

ACT II

MĀDHAVYA, THE JESTER: What a life. I'm sick and tired of being friends with this king who's addicted to hunting. We've been wandering from forest to forest, yelling 'DEER!', 'BOAR!', 'TIGER!' in the blazing heat of the summer afternoon, that, too, where there's no tree shade. We drink disgusting mountain water, bitter from gathered leaves. For the most part, we eat meat directly off the spit, at odd hours. I can't even sleep at night, disjointed from hours hunting on horseback. And then, right at dawn, I'm woken up way too early by the din of hunters—sonsofbitches—with a pack of hounds, taking over the forest. The pain doesn't stop there … think of a pimple on top of a boil! By my bad luck, yesterday, the king, leaving us behind, chasing a deer, entering an āśrama, saw a hermit-girl called Śakuntalā. After that, he doesn't even mention going back to town. Even today, he opened his eyes thinking only of her. What to do? I'll look for him after he gets ready. (*Walking, and looking*) What's this, the king, surrounded by attendant women wearing garlands of wildflowers, bow in hand. Okay. I'll stand here as if spent, limbs out of joint. This might earn me a break… (*Stands, leaning on a staff*)

(*The king enters, as described*)

DUṢYANTA: (*To himself*)

> Not easy to get, beloved,
> but the sight of her feelings
> consoles the heart
>
> Heart's desire's
> unsatiated, but mutual
> longing makes it pleasured

(*Smiling*) That's how the seeking-lover is mocked, even as he imagines that the mind of the loved one reflects his own wishes.

That she looked tenderly though really looking
somewhere else

Her gait seems flirtatious
But it's really the voluptuous behind
that makes it slow

That she spoke irritably
when her good friend chided
'Don't go'

All that's for my sake, thinks a lover
The lover thinks everything's about him

MĀDHAVYA: (*Standing in the same place*) My hands and legs can't move. I greet you with just words. Hullo, hullo.

DUṢYANTA: (*Smiling*) Why are your limbs paralysed?

MĀDHAVYA: Why, you hurt my eyes, then ask what's the reason for my tears!

DUṢYANTA: I don't get it.

MĀDHAVYA: The cane-plant that imitates a hunchback … is that from its own influence, or the river's force?

DUṢYANTA: There the cause is the river's force.

MĀDHAVYA: Mine too.

DUṢYANTA: How?

MĀDHAVYA: Leaving your job as king, should you behave like a jungle-dweller in a dreary place? The truth is, by chasing wild beasts, I'm no longer in command of my limbs, tortured at the joints. Humour me, let's take a break, at least for a day.

DUṢYANTA: (*To himself*) He said so too. As I think of Kaṇva's daughter, my mind's tired of the chase too.

I'm not able to arch
my bow—an arrow on it

at the deer who—as if—by living together
taught my sweetheart

how to glance

MĀDHAVYA: (*Looking at the king's face*) He muses over something within his heart, and my situation is not much more than a cry in the wilderness.

DUṢYANTA: What else. 'A friend's statement should not be opposed'—I stay put.

MĀDHAVYA: Take care! (*Wants to leave*)

DUṢYANTA: Stay, tell me more.

MĀDHAVYA: Do say.

DUṢYANTA: When you've rested, you need to help me with a little task that won't stress you out.

MĀDHAVYA: Like eating sweet dumplings? This happy occasion's welcome!

DUṢYANTA: I'll let you know. Who's there?

(*Guard Raivataka enters*)

RAIVATAKA: Yes, Sir, say.

DUṢYANTA: Raivataka, call the Army Chief.

RAIVATAKA: Yes. (*Leaves; re-enters with Bhadrasena, the Army Chief*) The king looks your way, about to say something. Go to him.

BHADRASEṆA: (*Sees the king*) Although hunting is considered harmful, it's all good in the king's case. Look at him:

Like a mountain-roving tusker
carries its spirit

Enduring sunrays without
a drop of sweat

A tough torso from
bowstring drawn nonstop

Can't quite tell how gaunt the limbs
So muscular

(*Approaches*) Wild beasts have been caught in the forest. Why does the king stay away?

DUṢYANTA: My enthusiasm for the hunt has been crushed by Mādhavya's mockery.

BHADRASENA: (*Aside to Mādhavya*) Be strong in your resistance. And I'll follow the King's inclinations. (*Aloud*) This fool babbles, but you set an example.

Fat burned, belly taut, slim, body fit for action
Learns about fear and anger in creatures' minds
When arrows make a moving target, the archer's buzz …

People lie: 'hunting's a waste'—
Where else is this much fun?

MĀDHAVYA: (*Angrily*) Get lost, O' great motivator, the king has returned to himself now. Roaming from jungle to jungle, you'll fall into the mouth of some old bear greedy for the nose of a man.

DUṢYANTA: Commander, we are near the āśrama, so I don't appreciate your words. For now:

Let buffaloes wallow in dirty water
splashing their horns at it
again and again

Let deer-herds gather in the shade
to ruminate

Let lots of boars relax
by the Muṣta-grass pools

And let this unstrung bow
take a break

BHADRASENA: As the king commands.

DUṢYANTA: So call back the hunters who went ahead. Let my soldiers who surround the hermitage be forbidden to hunt. See:

Tranquillity seems the theme
in people whose equity's
meditation

The power's hidden
Fiery

Like sun-stones cool to the touch
Spew their true nature when struck
by luminous others

BHADRASENA: Whatever the king commands.

MĀDHAVYA: You've made it free of flies. Now please sit in the shade of this tree entwined with a thick spread of vines. I'll sit too, relaxed.

DUṢYANTA: You go first.

MĀDHAVYA: This way. (*Both walk a little and sit down*)

DUṢYANTA: Mādhavya, your sight has not had its fill, you haven't seen what's worthy of seeing.

MĀDHAVYA: Why, but you're right before me!

DUṢYANTA: Everyone sees what they're fond of. I speak about her, Śakuntalā, the jewel of the āśrama.

MĀDHAVYA: (*To himself*) Okay, I won't give him a chance. (*Aloud*) You've got your sights on a hermit-girl who's beyond reach, eh?

DUṢYANTA: A Paurava's mind is never drawn to a forbidden object.

MĀDHAVYA: How so?

DUṢYANTA:

Like a Navamallikā flower
dropped loose
on an Arka leaf

Born to a divine woman—
Adopted by a sage—
Abandoned, found

MĀDHAVYA: Like someone tired of sweet dates craves for sour tamarind, you who've had the finest of women, now going after this…

DUṢYANTA: You argue like this because you haven't seen her.

MĀDHAVYA: She must be beautiful if she makes you so wonder-struck.

DUṢYANTA: Why go on?

Was she placed in an image
Then imagined to life?

Was Beauty heaped up
Then shaped by
the creator's mind?

When I think
of his creative power
and her form

She seems to outshine
creation's finest women

MĀDHAVYA: In that case, all the beauties are now put to shame!

DUṢYANTA: And this is also on my mind:

Flower not smelt
Sprout not snipped by fingernails
Gem not pierced
Fresh honey, not yet tasted

Her form flawless
An undivided reward
for good deeds

Who knows who
will ravish her, who will
destiny give this to

MĀDHAVYA: Then rescue her so she won't fall into the hands of some Iṅgudi hair oil grease-head jungle-camper.

DUṢYANTA: She's a dependent woman, and the guru is not here.

MĀDHAVYA: Do her eyes express inner feelings for you?

DUṢYANTA: Hermit-girls are not forward by nature. Yet—

Averted her eyes when I faced her
Smile, a hint at some other meaning
Behaviour checked by modesty
Love neither displayed nor hid

MĀDHAVYA: You mean she didn't sit in your lap the moment she saw you?

DUṢYANTA: As she was leaving with her friends her feelings towards me were rather obvious—shyly, of course.

A few steps, and the girl stopped, abrupt,
'Ouch, my foot! Pricked by a leaf'

Then lingered, face turned
towards me, open

Disentangling her not-at-all-entangled bark-dress
from branches of shrubs

MĀDHAVYA: Stock up on supplies then. I see you've turned the meditation forest into a pleasure garden.

DUṢYANTA: Mādhavya, I'm known to some of the hermits. Think, with what excuse can we go to the āśrama?

MĀDHAVYA: What other excuse? Are you not the king?

DUṢYANTA: So what?

MĀDHAVYA: Say 'Give us a sixth part of the rice harvest as tax.'

DUṢYANTA: Fool, in return for protecting them, they pay a tax worth more than heaps of precious gems. See:

Finite, the king's yield
from the four classes

Infinite, the sixth part of penance
ascetics give us

VOICES BACKSTAGE: We've found it!

DUṢYANTA: (*Listening*) From their steady, calm voices, I can tell they must be ascetics.

(*Raivataka enters*)

RAIVATAKA: Greetings, King. Two young hermits are at the door.

DUṢYANTA: Bring them in without delay.

RAIVATAKA: I'll usher them in. (*Leaves, and re-enters with the two young hermits*) Here they are, Sir.

(*Both see the king*)

BOTH: Wow, although illustrious, his personality inspires trust. Or rather, the king is not too different from our ascetics in that. Because:

In this chosen life-stage,
useful to all

Protection's his yoga, it
collects the same merit
penance does

Self-controlled, he's praised
to the skies in the songs
of celestial couples,

called 'sage', a sacred epithet,
—'king' is just a prefix

SECOND HERMIT: Gautama, is this Duṣyanta, friend of Indra?

FIRST HERMIT: Who else!

SECOND HERMIT:

Not surprising, this king,

arms long as city-gate beams
possesses solo

the entire earth up to
its cloud-blue horizons

thanks to his strung bow
and Indra's thunder

the gods hope for victory
in the war with demons

BOTH: Blessings, King.

DUṢYANTA: Greetings to you both.

BOTH: Be well. (*They offer fruit*)

DUṢYANTA: (*Receives with folded hands*) I'd like to know your orders.

BOTH: The āśrama residents have come to know that you're here. They request...

DUṢYANTA: What do they command...

BOTH: Because of Sage Kaṇva's absence, demons will make trouble for the fire rituals there. So, they request you, along with your charioteer, to preside over the āśrama for some nights.

DUṢYANTA: I'm honoured.

MĀDHAVYA: (*Aside*) Now their request is convenient...

DUṢYANTA: (*Smiles*) Raivataka, on my behalf, tell the charioteer to bring the chariot, and quiver with arrows.

RAIVATAKA: As the king commands.

BOTH: (*Happily*)

> Pauravas, donors of fearlessness
> in ritual sessions
>
> To follow your ancestors' example
> An apt course for you

DUṢYANTA: (*With folded hands*) You both may carry on. I'll come soon too.

BOTH: Do well. (*They leave*)

DUṢYANTA: Mādhavya, any curiosity to see Śakuntalā?

MĀDHAVYA: Well, initially, it was a flood. Now at the news of demons, not a drop's left!

DUṢYANTA: Don't be afraid. You'll be near me.

MĀDHAVYA: Then I'm saved from the demons!

(*Raivataka enters*)

RAIVATAKA: The chariot's ready for the king to take off. Karabhaka has also arrived from town with orders from the queen.

DUṢYANTA: (*Respectfully*) What, sent by my mother?

RAIVATAKA: Yes.

DUṢYANTA: You may bring him in.

RAIVATAKA: Sure. (*Leaves, and re-enters with Karabhaka*) Here's the king. Go near.

KARABHAKA: (*Approaches*) Greetings, King. The queen commands: 'My religious fast will conclude on the fourth day to come. It should be in the presence of my son who has a long life.'

DUṢYANTA: Here, duty towards the hermits. There, mother's command. Can't cross the line on either. What's the right choice here?

MĀDHAVYA: Float in space like Triśaṅku!

DUṢYANTA: I'm worried, for sure.

> Because the two tasks are
> in two different places
>
> My mind's divided
> in two like a
>
> River, its flow checked
> by a mountain

(*Thinks*) Mādhavya, you're considered a son to my mother. So you leave from here now, tell the queen of my engagement in the work of the hermitage, you take my place in the ritual duties of a son.

MĀDHAVYA: I hope you don't think I'm scared of demons!

DUṢYANTA: (*Smiling*) Oh, how's that possible, for a great brahmin?

MĀDHAVYA: I'll go as a king's younger brother ought to.

DUṢYANTA: Why, I'll send all my followers with you, saying it's to avoid the disturbance to the forest.

MĀDHAVYA: (*With pride*) That makes me a prince!

DUṢYANTA: (*To himself*) This is a fickle fellow. He might talk about my longing in the queens' quarters. Maybe I should portray the situation differently … (*Taking Mādhavya by hand, aloud*) Listen, my friend, I'm going to the āśrama because of the respect I have for the sages. In real fact, I have no desire for the hermit-girl. See:

> Where are we, and where's she …
> A stranger, raised with fawns
>
> Words spoken in jest, don't
> take them seriously

MĀDHAVYA: Okay.

(*Everyone leaves*)

END OF ACT II

ACT III

A student of the patron of the vedic rituals enters, carrying Darbha grass.

STUDENT: Oh superpowerful King Duṣyanta. The king simply enters the āśrama, and our rituals get done there without disturbances.

Who needs a mounted arrow?
With a slight twang

from a distant bowstring
He shoos away dangers

It's as if the bow roared
ferocious

Now I'll give the Ṛgvedic priests this Darbha grass to scatter on the fire-platform. (*Walks, and looks*) Priyaṃvadā, for whom are you carrying the lotus leaves and pulpy lotus root? To rub on whom? (*Mimes listening*) What do you say? Śakuntalā's very ill from being out in the sun? To cool her body? Go quickly then. She's the life-breath of the head of the family, Sage Kaṇva. And I will send some sacred water with Gautamī to cool Śakuntalā.

END OF PRELUDE

(*The king enters in a lovelorn condition*)

DUṢYANTA: (*Sighs*)

I know the power of ascetics
I know that girl is not free

But I still can't control this—
My heart

Kāma, you're armed with flowers … both you and the moon betray the trust of lovers. Because:

> Your floral arrows—
> Moon's cool rays—
>
> Both false
> in my case
>
> From an icy womb the moon
> delivers fire-rays, you too
>
> make your floral arrows
> diamond-hard

Or

> Relentless the heartache
> dolphin-bannered Kāma brings, but
>
> If he hurls his arrows for her, the woman with
> intoxicating eyes, he's welcome

(*Walks about, disturbed*) The ascetics' rituals are done, I've been let go, I'm stressed, where shall I take a break?

There's no rest in anything but in the sight of my love. I'll look for her. (*Notices the sun*) Most likely, Śakuntalā spends this burning hot time of day with her friends under the shade of thick vines on the banks of river Mālinī. (*Walks around, mimes the sensation of touch*) Oh this place is nice because of the breeze.

> Can do!
>
> Limbs festering in Kāma's heat
> can embrace
>
> the breeze, lotus-scented carrier of spray
> from river Mālinī's waves

(*Walks and looks*) She has to be nearby, in this alcove of vines surrounded by cane plants. As I thought …

> Seen in the white sand
> at this gate, a row
>
> Fresh footprints
>
> Raised in the front
> At the back, deeper
>
> from heavy hips

I'll look through the branches then. (*Goes, does so. Says happily*) Ha! Nirvāṇa for my eyes! Here's the love of my heart lying on a flowerbed on a stone slab, with her friends. I'll listen to their private talk. (*Stands thinking this*)

(*Śakuntalā enters with two friends, busy as noted*)

TWO FRIENDS: (*Fanning affectionately*) Hey Śakuntalā, does the breeze from the lotus-leaf-fan please you?

ŚAKUNTALĀ: Are you fanning me?

(*Both friends look at each other in despair*)

DUṢYANTA: Śakuntalā looks seriously ill. (*Takes a guess*) Is this because of heat? Or is it like the state of my own heart? (*With hope*) Enough with negativity!

> Uśīra paste on her breasts
> The one lotus-stalk bracelet loosened
>
> Beloved's body, racked, but
> Desirable
>
> Similar to the heat of love
> Hot weather's effects

But this charming culpability in young women—
No, not from summer heat

PRIYAṂVADĀ: Anasūyā, Śakuntalā seems restless from the moment she first set sight on the great king. Is it possible her affliction is due to that?

ANASŪYĀ: My mind has the same doubt. Let it be. I'll ask her about it. (*Aloud, to Śakuntalā*) Śakuntalā, I have to ask you something. Your suffering seems terrible.

ŚAKUNTALĀ: (*Sits up*) Anasūyā, what do you want to ask me?

ANASŪYĀ: Śakuntalā, we are uninitiated in matters of love. But, we see your state is just like that of the lovesick people we've heard about in legends. Say, what's the reason for your suffering? Without knowing the reason for sickness, there can be no cure.

DUṢYANTA: My suspicion is in line with Anasūyā's. What I thought was not prejudiced by my own state.

ŚAKUNTALĀ: (*To herself*) My feelings are intense. Even so, I'm not able to confess to them so abruptly.

PRIYAṂVADĀ: (*To Śakuntalā*) Śakuntalā, what she says is right. Why ignore your problem? With every day your limbs are wasting away. Only the shadow of your beauty does not forsake you.

DUṢYANTA: Priyaṃvadā speaks the truth. That's what it's like:

For a face, a wasted cheek
Breasts no longer firm at the chest
Waist thinner than ever
Shoulders droop a lot
Complexion, wan

Looks sad and lovely lovesick

Like a Mādhavī vine
with wind-shrivelled leaves

ŚAKUNTALĀ: Who else will I tell? But I will be a burden to you.

ANASŪYĀ AND PRIYAṂVADĀ: That's why we insist. Grief is only tolerable when shared with close friends.

DUṢYANTA:

> Quizzed by friends who share
> joy and sorrow
>
> The girl cannot but reveal
> the reason for her state
>
> She gazed at me
> with longing, yet
>
> I'm nervous now to
> hear her response

ŚAKUNTALĀ: Because from when the good king fell before my sight…

ANASŪYĀ AND PRIYAṂVADĀ: Say, dear…

ŚAKUNTALĀ: … since then I've been in this state, with longing for him.

DUṢYANTA: (*Happily*) I've heard what had to be heard.

> Kāma caused my suffering
> Turns out, my saviour's he
>
> Like the day that brings us heat
> Also soothes us with rainclouds

ŚAKUNTALĀ: If you're willing, do that by which I am the object of the good king's pity. Or else, for sure sprinkle me with water and sesame seed, *the death ritual*.

DUṢYANTA: Words that end doubt.

PRIYAṂVADĀ: (*Aside*) Anasūyā, she's far gone with love, and cannot bear to lose time. He, to whom she feels attached, is the crown of the Puru race. It's appropriate that her desire should be approved.

ANASŪYĀ: As you say. (*Aloud*) Luckily, friend, your feelings are worthy of you. Where could a great river flow, except to the sea?

PRIYAṂVADĀ: What other than a mango tree can support a jasmine creeper?

DUṢYANTA: It's not a surprise when the two Viśākha stars of spring follow the moon's track, is it?

ANASŪYĀ: Priyaṃvadā, what's an idea by which we can attain our friend's wishes without delay, and in secret?

PRIYAṂVADĀ: 'Secretly' needs some thought. 'Quickly' is easy.

ANASŪYĀ: How come?

PRIYAṂVADĀ: These days the good king is sleepless and emaciated, and his feelings are betrayed by his tender glances towards Śakuntalā.

DUṢYANTA: Yes, I have become like that. So:

> Again and again I push back up
> my gold armlet that slips
>
> Slips, not even grazing
> the raised welt my bowstring made
> on my wrist
>
> Its gemstones discoloured
> by inner heat
> by hot tears
>
> flowing from the outer corners
> of my eyes that rest
> on my arms
>
> Night after night

PRIYAṂVADĀ: (*Thinks*) Let her write a love letter. On the pretext of giving him the remainder of the holy offerings, I will make it reach the king's hands, concealed in a flower.

ANASŪYĀ: I like this neat plan. What does Śakuntalā say?

ŚAKUNTALĀ: Why wouldn't I agree to your plan?

PRIYAṂVADĀ: First think of a statement about yourself, and then a well-worded letter.

ŚAKUNTALĀ: I'll think. But again, my heart trembles at the thought of his rejection.

DUṢYANTA: (*Happily*)

> I stand here, eager
> for union, but
>
> Timid, you suspect
> rejection
>
> A seeker may or may
> not get Fortune
>
> What Fortune wants, how
> can it be unavailable

ANASŪYĀ AND PRIYAṂVADĀ: Hmpf, you who don't have the confidence in your own merit, you'd now use the tip of a cloth to hide the healing moon!

ŚAKUNTALĀ: (*With a smile*) Now I stand corrected. (*Thinking thus, gets up*)

DUṢYANTA: I'll stay right here to watch my beloved with unblinking eyes.

> As she composes words
> She betrays her passion
> for me

One eyebrow raised like a
vine on her face

Goosebumps
on her cheek

ŚAKUNTALĀ: I've thought about the song, friends, but writing materials are not at hand.

PRIYAMṂVADĀ: Engrave the letters with your nails on this lotus leaf, smooth as a parrot's breast.

ŚAKUNTALĀ: (*Does as said*) Listen, friends, if this makes sense, or no.

ANASŪYĀ AND PRIYAMṂVADĀ: We're listening.

ŚAKUNTALĀ: (*Reads*)

Don't know what's in your heart,
cruel man, but

Day and night, love burns my limbs
that long for you.

DUṢYANTA: (*Rises suddenly*)

Slim girl, Love burns you,
But consumes me relentlessly

As the moon's wiped out by the day
Not the water lily

ANASŪYĀ AND PRIYAMṂVADĀ: (*Happily*) Heart's desire here without delay, well come!

(*Śakuntalā wants to get up*)

DUṢYANTA: Relax …

Your sore limbs at rest
On crushed flowers

Fragrant as fast-fading lotus-stalk bits
Don't need to follow formalities

ANASŪYĀ: Let our friend sit on a part of the stone slab.

(*The king sits. Shy, Śakuntalā stays where she is.*)

PRIYAṂVADĀ: Both of you, your passion for each other is evident to us. Friendship makes me speak redundantly.

DUṢYANTA: Good woman, that's not to be laughed at. When something intended is left unsaid, it causes suffering.

PRIYAṂVADĀ: This is a king's duty—to remove the suffering of his people.

DUṢYANTA: There is nothing more important than that.

PRIYAṂVADĀ: It is for you that our dear friend has been brought to this state by Kāma. Accordingly, you need to support her life.

DUṢYANTA: Good woman, our love is mutual. I feel honoured in every way.

ŚAKUNTALĀ: (*Looking at Priyaṃvadā*) Friends, why detain the king, who is anxious, bereft of his wives?

DUṢYANTA: Lovely one,

My heart, devoted
to none other

Intoxicating eyes, it's
you who's close
to my heart

If you think otherwise,
slain by Kāma's arrows, I am
slain again

ANASŪYĀ: Śakuntalā, it's known that kings have many lovers. Carry on in such a way that you don't become a source of grief to others in the family.

DUṢYANTA: Good woman, what's there to worry

Many wives, but two
anchors for my race

The earth surrounded by the ocean
And your friend.

ANASŪYĀ AND PRIYAṂVADĀ: We're satisfied.

PRIYAṂVADĀ: (*Casts a glance*) Anasūyā, this fawn looks eagerly for its mother here and there. Come, let's unite them. (*Both begin to leave*)

ŚAKUNTALĀ: I'm stranded! Either of you, come back!

ANASŪYĀ AND PRIYAṂVADĀ: He who's the protector of the earth is near you. (*They leave*)

ŚAKUNTALĀ: Why, they're gone!

DUṢYANTA: Don't panic. Isn't the person who adores you beside you?

O woman of shapely thighs,
Shall I

Fan you with lotus-leaf stalks
The moist, cool breeze easing your fatigue

Place your lotus-red feet on my lap
Massage them any which way you like?

ŚAKUNTALĀ: I won't offend those who deserve respect.

DUṢYANTA:

Hey Lovely one,
The day's young

Your body's in this state.
Your delicate limbs
So sore

How will you go
in this heat?

Leaving the flowerbed
And lotus leaves clothing
your breasts

(*Stops her by force*)

ŚAKUNTALĀ: Puru King, behave yourself. Although burning with love, I cannot be myself.

DUṢYANTA: Timid one, don't worry about elders. Seeing this, the head of the family, who is well-versed in dharma, will not find fault.

It's well known, many
daughters of great sages

First marry Gāndharva-style
Fathers approve later

ŚAKUNTALĀ: Let me go now. I'll take my friends' permission again.

DUṢYANTA: Okay. I'll free you.

ŚAKUNTALĀ: When?

DUṢYANTA: Lovely one,

When I, thirsty, seize gently
the flavour of your lips

As a bee does, a tender, new,
unspoilt blossom

(*He tries to raise her face, Śakuntalā squirms free*)

VOICE BACKSTAGE: Bride goose, say bye to your mate! Night's here.

ŚAKUNTALĀ: (*Listens, confused*) Puru King, for sure Gautamī-Ma comes here to ask after my health. Get behind the tree!

DUṢYANTA: Fine. (*Hides himself*)

(*Gautamī, with a pot in hand, and friends enter*)

FRIENDS: This way, this way, Gautamī.

GAUTAMĪ: Śakuntalā, are your sore limbs better?

ŚAKUNTALĀ: Somewhat better.

GAUTAMĪ: Your body will definitely be relieved from pain with this Darbha-grass water.

(*They begin to leave*)

ŚAKUNTALĀ: (*To herself*) When things were easy for you at the outset, you didn't let go of fear. Why worry about separation now? Now that things have moved on, why worry now? (*Stops after a step*) Bower of vines who took away my suffering, I say bye to you now, to enjoy when we meet again. (*Śakuntalā leaves with others*)

DUṢYANTA: (*Returns to his earlier position, sighs*) The achievement of objects of desire is fraught with obstacles.

Lower lip barred again
by fingers

Faltering words of protest—
Charming!

Turning her face
with long eyelashes,

I raised it—oh how
did I not kiss it!

Where do I go now? Or, do I stay for a while in this bower of vines that my darling has enjoyed and left?

This—the flowery stone-bed
pressed by her body

This—the faded love-letter
inscribed on a lotus leaf
with fingernails

This—the ornament of lotus-stalks
slipped from her arms

My eyes cling thus
I cannot leave abruptly

This bower of reeds
Though empty

VOICE IN THE SKY: King,

Evening rituals begin

Flesh-eating demons
Cloud-demons
Fall around the lit altar

Terrorizing shadows roam

DUṢYANTA: Here I come. (*Leaves*)

END OF ACT III

ACT IV

(*Śakuntalā's two friends enter, gathering flowers*)

ANASŪYĀ: Priyaṃvadā, my mind's relaxed that Śakuntalā's gone to a suitable husband in the Gāndharva style … and yet, there's some reason to be worried.

PRIYAṂVADĀ: Why?

ANASŪYĀ: Sent off by the ascetics after the vedic sacrifice today, returning to his own city, going into his wives' rooms, will the king remember what transpired here, or won't he…

PRIYAṂVADĀ: Relax. People who look so good don't have a bad character. But I have no idea what Father will think, hearing this news now.

ANASŪYĀ: As I see it, it should have his approval.

PRIYAṂVADĀ: Why?

ANASŪYĀ: The most important wish—a daughter must be given to a man of good character. If that's accomplished by destiny, isn't the father's desire achieved without any effort?

PRIYAṂVADĀ: (*Sees the flower basket*) Enough flowers collected for worship.

ANASŪYĀ: We must worship our dear friend Śakuntalā's guardian-deity.

PRIYAṂVADĀ: Agree.

(*They begin the worship*)

DURVĀSA'S VOICE BACKSTAGE: Ahem. I am here.

ANASŪYĀ: Sounds like the announcement of a guest.

PRIYAMVADĀ: Śakuntalā's near the hut. (*To herself*) Though mentally absent right now.

ANASŪYĀ: Okay, enough flowers. (*Both start to leave*)

DURVĀSA'S VOICE BACKSTAGE: Argh, you insult a guest!

You don't realize
my yogic power.

He whom you obsess over

Like a drunk who doesn't
remember the backstory,

Won't remember you
even when prodded.

PRIYAMVADĀ: Oh no! Something awful has happened. Empty-headed, Śakuntalā has offended someone who calls for respect. And this is not just a nobody. This is Durvāsa, the sage who gets angry easily. After cursing, he's stomping back, unstoppably, making wild gestures. Who other than Fire can burn?

ANASŪYĀ: Go! Fall at his feet and make him come back. Meanwhile I'll get some water to offer him.

PRIYAMVADĀ: Okay. (*Leaves*)

ANASŪYĀ: (*Steps falter*) Oh! Because of my hasty stumbling, the flower basket has dropped from my hand.

(*Priyaṃvadā enters*)

PRIYAMVADĀ: Whose pleas will he listen to, twisted as he is? But I pacified him a little.

ANASŪYĀ: (*Smiles*) Big achievement in this case … do tell!

PRIYAṂVADĀ: When he didn't want to come back, I pleaded: 'Sir, seeing as it's a first-time offence, consider her a daughter who's ignorant of your yogic power, forgive her.'

ANASŪYĀ: And then?

PRIYAṂVADĀ: Saying, 'My word cannot be otherwise'—and then pronouncing—'on looking at an object of remembrance, the curse will be cancelled'—he vanished.

ANASŪYĀ: Now it's possible to breathe. There's that ring engraved with his name which the king himself put on her when leaving, saying 'remember'. Because of that, Śakuntalā will have a solution under her control.

PRIYAṂVADĀ: Come, let's complete our worship to the deities.

(*They walk around*)

PRIYAṂVADĀ: Look there, face cupped in her left hand, our Śakuntalā looks like a picture. She's not even conscious of herself, thinking of her husband who has left. As for guests!

ANASŪYĀ: Priyaṃvadā, let our lips be sealed about this incident. Our Śakuntalā, delicate by nature, must be protected.

PRIYAṂVADĀ: Who will sprinkle a Navamallikā with hot water!

(*Both leave*)

END OF INTERLUDE

(*A disciple who has just woken up enters*)

DISCIPLE: I've been asked, by Kaṇva who's back from his trip, to find out what time it is. I'll see how much of night's left, by going outdoors. (*Walks and looks*)

> On one side,
> the husband of herbs *the Moon*
> sets on the mount

On the other, the Sun,
ushered by red dawn
his charioteer

The rise and fall of
these two luminaries

Warns the world
of its changing fate

What's more:

The very same lotus pond
When the moon is hid
Does not please my eyes, its
beauty, a matter of memory.

When the lover's absent
the grief of women must
—weak as they are—be
quite unbearable.

(*Drawing the curtain, Anasūyā enters*)

ANASŪYĀ: Even someone detached from worldly matters can't help but know how badly the king has behaved with Śakuntalā.

DISCIPLE: I'll tell the teacher it's time for the vedic ritual.

ANASŪYĀ: Though wide awake, what to do? Hands and legs don't move for regular daily routine. Let Kāma win. By whose false company pure-hearted Śakuntalā gave her word. Or it's Durvāsa's curse, that turns. Otherwise how come the king, having sworn like that, doesn't even send a letter? So we might send his ring of remembrance. Who can we ask among the pathetic ascetics? Though I think the blame goes to our friend, I can't go so far as to inform father Kaṇva, who's back from his trip, about Śakuntalā, Duṣyanta's wife, and pregnant. What's to be done in this situation?

PRIYAṂVADĀ: (*Enters, happily*) Hurry up, hurry up, get started on the celebration of Śakuntalā's departure.

ANASŪYĀ: How's that so?

PRIYAṂVADĀ: Listen. I went to Śakuntalā to ask if she slept well. There, as her head hung shyly, she was blessed by father Kaṇva himself, thus—'Luckily, the patron's offering fell right into the vedic fire although his vision was obscured by smoke. Śakuntalā, like knowledge given to a good student, you've proven to be no worry. I'll send you today to your husband's side, protected by ascetics.'

ANASŪYĀ: But who told father Kaṇva the news?

PRIYAṂVADĀ: A disembodied voice, in meter, when he entered the vedic-fire room.

> Be aware brahmin,
>
> As the Śamī tree carries Fire
> Your daughter bears
>
> A glorious seed
> fathered by Duṣyanta
>
> For the welfare of the world

ANASŪYĀ: (*Hugs Priyaṃvadā*) I'm happy. But, that she's sent right away, today … I feel both a little choked, and happy.

PRIYAṂVADĀ: We'll bear the sadness lightly. Let the suffering girl be at ease.

ANASŪYĀ: I've kept a Kesara garland that stays fresh a long time in the coconut basket hanging on that mango tree branch. Perfect for such an occasion. Take that in your hand now. I'll gather musk too, sacred clay, Durva-grass shoots and other such nice decorations.

PRIYAṂVADĀ: Do so.

(*Anasūyā leaves, Priyaṃvadā gathers flowers*)

VOICE BACKSTAGE: Gautamī, ask Śārṅgarava to escort Śakuntalā.

PRIYAṂVADĀ: Anasūyā! Hurry up. They're summoning ascetics who will go to Hastinapura.

(*Anasūyā enters, with hands full of materials*)

ANASŪYĀ: Come, let's go.

(*They walk around*)

PRIYAṂVADĀ: (*Looks*) Here's Śakuntalā, after an early morning head-bath, accompanied by ascetic women blessing her with Nīvāra rice grains in their holy hands, wishing her well. Let's go near them.

(*They go forward*)

(*Śakuntalā is seated, surrounded by Gautamī and other ascetic women*)

FIRST ASCETIC WOMAN: (*To Śakuntalā*) Śakuntalā, may you get the title of Chief Queen, which shows your husband's regard for you.

SECOND ASCETIC WOMAN: Śakuntalā, may you become the mother of a hero.

THIRD ASCETIC WOMAN: Śakuntalā, may your husband think highly of you.

(*Giving such blessings, everyone leaves except Gautamī*)

ANASŪYĀ AND PRIYAṂVADĀ: (*Approach*) The joys of a holy bath to you.

ŚAKUNTALĀ: Welcome. Sit here.

ANASŪYĀ AND PRIYAṂVADĀ: (*Bring the platters with auspicious stuff, sit*) Śakuntalā, get ready, we'll dress you up with auspicious stuff.

ŚAKUNTALĀ: This is a great honour. Being dressed by my friends will be rare in the future. (*Sheds tears*)

ANASŪYĀ AND PRIYAṂVADĀ: It's not appropriate to cry on this happy occasion. (*They wipe her tears and decorate her*)

PRIYAṂVADĀ: This beauty deserves jewellery. We're not doing justice to it with what's available at the āśrama.

(*Two ascetic boys, Nārada and Gautama, enter with presents*)

NĀRADA AND GAUTAMA: Here's jewellery. Let her be decked up.

(*Everyone's surprised to see them*)

GAUTAMĪ: Nārada, my boy, where's this from?

NĀRADA: From the power of Father Kaṇva.

GAUTAMĪ: Did he materialize them?

GAUTAMA: Oh no. Listen. We were told by him, 'Fetch flowers from the trees for Śakuntalā'. Then this:

> From some tree appeared a new
> auspicious, moon-white silk robe.
>
> From some tree a free outpouring
> of lac juice to stain feet
>
> From the hands of other forest deities,
> their upper halves surfacing,
>
> jostling with new shoots,
> gifts of jewellery.

PRIYAṂVADĀ: This production points to the good fortune you'll experience in your husband's house.

(*Śakuntalā looks coy*)

NĀRADA: Gautama, come here. Let's tell Kaṇva who's coming from his bath about the work of the trees.

GAUTAMA: Okay.

(*Both leave*)

ANASŪYĀ AND PRIYAṂVADĀ: Oh dear, we folks have never used ornaments. We'll deck your limbs based on what we've seen in paintings.

ŚAKUNTALĀ: I know your talent!

(*Both decorate her*)

(*Bathed, Kaṇva enters*)

KAṆVA:

> 'Śakuntalā goes today'—
> My heart feels it
>
> Tears repressed
> Throat choked
> Eyes glazed
> Tension …
>
> If foster love takes me who lives in the forest
> to such a fragile state
>
> Imagine how hard a householder is hit
> on first parting with a daughter.

(*Walks around*)

FRIENDS: Śakuntalā, you're all set. Now put on the pair of silk garments.

(*Śakuntalā gets up and puts them on*)

GAUTAMĪ: Here's father, eyes flowing with tears, as if hugging you. Receive him.

ŚAKUNTALĀ: (*Shy*) Greetings, Father.

KAṆVA:

Be adored by your husband
As Śarmiṣṭhā was by Yayāti

Beget a son Emperor
As she did King Puru

GAUTAMĪ: Sir, this is not just a blessing, it's a boon.

KAṆVA: Śakuntalā, go around the vedic fire.

(*All walk around*)

KAṆVA: (*Blesses her with a Ṛgveda hymn*)

Neatly round a centre platform
With sacred grass scattered surround
Blaze vedic fires
May the fragrance of the offerings
Delete your sins
May these vedic fires purify you

Now get going. Where are Śārṅgarava and the others?

(*Disciple Śārṅgarava enters*)

ŚĀRṄGARAVA: Here we are, Sir.

KAṆVA: Show your sister the way.

ŚĀRṄGARAVA: This way, Sister, this way.

(*All walk around*)

KAṆVA:

Won't drink water before you

Loves to prettify, but
likes you, so won't
pluck a sprig

Your first flowering's
celebration for her

It is she who goes, Śakuntalā,
to her husband's house

Everyone, give her leave to go

(*Listens to a cuckoo sing*)

The trees, Śakuntalā's friends
who live in the forest, said 'yes'
with this, the chirruping
of a cuckoo

VOICE IN THE SKY:

May there be

Lotus lakes, pleasant
green spots

Shady trees tempering
hot sunrays

A cool, calm, breeze
The dust, lily-pollen soft

Safe journey!

(*Everyone listens, surprised*)

GAUTAMĪ: You've been given leave to go by the deities of the forest—close, familiar friends. Say bye to them.

ŚAKUNTALĀ: (*Folded hands, walks around*) Priyaṃvadā, I'm keen to see him, but my feet fall ahead with the sadness of leaving the āśrama.

PRIYAṂVADĀ: It's not only my friend who has separation-angst. Even the forest seems that way at your forthcoming departure.

> Dancing peacocks pause
> Deer drop cud
>
> Vines shed dry leaves
> like tears

ŚAKUNTALĀ: (*Remembers*) Father, I'll say bye to my Vanajyotsnā, my vine-sister.

KAṆVA: I know your sisterly fondness for her. Here, to your right.

ŚAKUNTALĀ: (*Goes near the vine*) Vanajyotsnā, though you're paired with the mango tree, hug me back with your branches which are on this side. From today, I'll be far from you.

KAṆVA:

> By your fortune you've got
> An apt husband
>
> Whom I had in mind for you
> from the outset
>
> The Navamallikā vine leans
> on the mango tree …
>
> I'm unworried now
> for her, and you
>
> Carry on your way now

ŚAKUNTALĀ: (*To both friends*) Friends, she's placed in both your hands.

ANASŪYĀ AND PRIYAṂVADĀ: In whose care are we placed? (*They cry*)

KAṆVA: Anasūyā, enough of crying. It's by you both that Śakuntalā needs to be steadied.

(*Everyone walks around*)

ŚAKUNTALĀ: Father, this doe that grazes near the hut, the one that's slow from pregnancy, when she has a healthy delivery, send a messenger with the good news.

KAṆVA: I won't forget.

ŚAKUNTALĀ: (*Her walk, obstructed*) Who's that tugging at my skirts?

KAṆVA: Darling,

> This deer who does not budge
> from your path, you rubbed
>
> oil of Iṅgudi fruit on mouth blisters
> he got from grass pricks
>
> You raised with handfuls
> of Śyāmaka grains
>
> Your foster son
> It's him

ŚAKUNTALĀ: My dear, why follow me who's forsaking friends? I raised you soon after your birth, when you were without your mother. Now, without me around, my father will care for you. So turn back. (*Cries, leaves*)

KAṆVA:

Steady, control the flow of tears
held in your long-lashed eyes

Not seeing this path's uneven ground
Your steps falter

ŚĀRṄGARAVA: According to tradition, follow someone close only up to the water's edge. Here's the lake's edge. Say your bit here and go back.

KAṆVA: Then we'll shelter in the shade of the milk-tree.

(*They all walk around, and stop*)

KAṆVA: (*To himself*) What's the right message I must send Duṣyanta?

ŚAKUNTALĀ: Friend, see! The Cakravāka bird cries, 'I'm having a hard time'—not seeing its partner hidden in the lotus leaf.

ANASŪYĀ: Don't say that.

Yes she spends a long, bereft night
without her lover, but

Though the grief of separation's deep
Hope's the rope that helps

KAṆVA: Śārṅgarava, presenting Śakuntalā to the king, you must say these words from me.

ŚĀRṄGARAVA: Tell me, Sir.

KAṆVA:

Consider
my yogic wealth

Consider
your high lineage

Consider how
spontaneous her fondness for you
unarranged by family

She must be regarded equal
to your wives

Beyond that depends on fate.

In that, the wife's relatives
have no say.

ŚĀRṄGARAVA: Got it.

KAṆVA: Darling, time to advise you. Though I live in the forest, I know the ways of the world.

ŚĀRṄGARAVA: There's nothing the wise don't know.

KAṆVA: When you've arrived at your husband's house:

Revere elders. Befriend co-wives.
Don't be cross if your husband provokes you

To servants, be generous
To good fortune, indifferent

That's the way young women become
mistresses of the house.

Otherwise a disgrace to the race.

What does Gautamī think?

GAUTAMĪ: That's the guidance for a wife. Śakuntalā, take all that in.

KAṆVA: Hug me, and your friends.

ŚAKUNTALĀ: Father, do Priyaṃvadā and the others have to turn around from here?

KAṆVA: Darling, they too must be given in marriage. It's not appropriate for them to go there. Gautamī will go with you.

ŚAKUNTALĀ: (*Hugs her father*) Now how can I, away from my father's lap, take on a life in another place? Like a sandal plant uprooted from the slopes of Malaya mountain?

KAṆVA: Why so nervous?

In the role of housewife to an eminent husband
Ever-busy with his important work

Delivering a good son soon
Like the eastern horizon, the sun

Darling, you won't call
the separation from me,

sorrow.

(*Śakuntalā falls at her father's feet*)

KAṆVA: What I wish, may it be realized.

ŚAKUNTALĀ: (*Approaches her friends*) Both of you hug me together!

FRIENDS: (*Hugging Śakuntalā*) If the king is slow to remember you, then show this ring engraved with his own name.

ŚAKUNTALĀ: I shudder at your doubt.

FRIENDS: Don't be afraid. Blame the doubt on excessive love.

ŚĀRṄGARAVA: The sun has moved to another region. Hurry now.

ŚAKUNTALĀ: (*Stands facing the āśrama*) Father, when will I see the āśrama again?

KAṆVA: Listen.

After a long, long time
As co-wife of the vast earth

Duṣyanta's unbeatable son
Enthroned, given

The kingdom's duties
by your husband

You'll come together
to this peaceful āśrama

GAUTAMĪ: Śakuntalā, the time to go slips by. Send your father back. Or he will keep saying the same thing again and again. (*To Kaṇva*) Please go.

KAṆVA: Darling, it's getting late for the rituals.

ŚAKUNTALĀ: (*Hugs her father again*) My father's body is emaciated by penance. Don't worry too much about me.

KAṆVA: (*With a sigh*)

How can my sorrow ease
When I see

The Nīvāra grains you
once scattered

Growing
at the cottage door.

Go. Safe journey.

(*Śakuntalā and her fellow travellers leave*)

FRIENDS: Oh no! Śakuntalā's hidden by the forest.

KAṆVA: (*With a sigh*) Anasūyā, your dhārmic companion has gone. Control your grief, follow me, I'm on my way.

ANASŪYĀ AND PRIYAṂVADĀ: How can we enter the āśrama? It's empty without Śakuntalā.

KAṆVA: Friendship makes you feel that way. (*Walks around, thoughtful*) Oh I feel good after sending Śakuntalā to her husband's house. How …

Sending her home today I feel
Clear within, as if I

Returned a deposit.
A girl belongs to another.

(*Everyone leaves*)

END OF ACT IV

ACT V

(*The king, seated with the jester; two female guards, Vetravatī and Pratihārī, on the side.)*

MĀDHAVYA: (*Listens*) Listen, in the music hall. Hear, a clear sound, melody, a song. I guess Hamsapādikā Ma'am is practising music.

DUṢYANTA: Sshh, so I can hear.

|| A SONG IN THE AIR ||

Hey bee, lusty
for fresh honey you

kissed the mango-blossom.
How you forget it!

Just by living with a lotus

DUṢYANTA: What a song, full of feeling.

MĀDHAVYA: Did you get the literal meaning of the song?

DUṢYANTA: (*Smiles*) She's someone I made love to once. I get it, this is her finding fault with me for loving Queen Vasumatī. Tell Hamsapādikā for me, I've been cleverly scolded!

MĀDHAVYA: Whatever. (*Gets up*) If she gets others to grab me by my hair, I'll have no hope for escape. Like a detached ascetic in the hands of an apsarā.

DUṢYANTA: Go. Pass on the message to her in a civilized manner.

MĀDHAVYA: What a fate. (*Leaves*)

DUṢYANTA: (*To himself*) I'm not separated from anyone I love. Why do I feel so strongly moved when I hear the meaning of the song?

Even a happy creature
becomes wistful

Seeing pleasing things
Hearing sweet sounds

Brings back to mind
Deep impressions

Unknown friendships
from another life

(*Remains disturbed*)

(*Chamberlain Kañcukī enters*)

KAÑCUKĪ: Argh, I've been reduced to this state.

The cane staff
I used to boss over
the king's harem

The same's a crutch
for my stumbling gait
as time passed by

Anyway, the king's dhārmic duties can't be passed over. Yet, I don't feel eager to inform him right now of the arrival of Kaṇva's disciples. It will tie him down again, he's just got off work.

The sun yoked his steeds
just once

The breeze blows
night and day

Always *serpent* Śeṣa holds
the weight of the world

That's a king's duty, for
he gets paid one-sixth *tax*

It goes with the territory.

So I'll do my job. (*Walks, and notices*) Here he is.

Ruling his people as his
own kids, weary at heart

he retreats to solitude.
Hot from grazing the herd

The head-elephant retires
to a cool spot

(*Approaches*) Some forest hermits living at the foot of the Himālaya mountain are here, bearing Kaṇva's message. They're with some women.

DUṢYANTA: (*Respectfully*) What, with a message from Kaṇva?

KAÑCUKĪ: No doubt.

DUṢYANTA: Tell teacher Somarāta on my behalf, 'Honour them with vedic rituals and welcome them personally'. I'll wait too, at a place fit to receive the hermits.

KAÑCUKĪ: As you say. (*Leaves*)

DUṢYANTA: (*Gets up*) Pratihārī, show the way to the vedic-fire room.

PRATIHĀRĪ: This way, this way, King.

DUṢYANTA: (*Walks around, looks tired, overworked*) All beings achieve happiness when they get desired objects. But suffering's at the heart of success for kings.

Achievement only takes
ambition away

Looking after what's acquired—
Nothing but bothersome

A kingdom's like an umbrella
you hold with your own hand

Stress, rather than
de-stress

TWO BARDS: (*Enter*) Morning, King!

FIRST:

Unmindful of your own comfort
you slave daily for world-welfare
That's your job.

The tree soothes the suffering of
those who shelter in its shade.
Feels the heat on its head.

SECOND:

With your power

You stop those on the wrong path
You stop arguments
You can protect

When there's no shortage of money
There's no shortage of friends
You're the friend for the rest

DUṢYANTA: I was mentally exhausted, I feel refreshed now. (*Walks around*)

PRATIHĀRĪ: Here's the porch of the vedic-fire room, just swept, nice. The vedic-cow's around. Step up, King.

DUṢYANTA: (*Climbs, leans on his attendant's shoulder*) Pratihārī, what did Sage Kaṇva want that he sent the ascetics to me?

Could it be …

The ongoing penance of ascetics
spoilt by problems

The animals in the holy forest,
abused by someone

Trees about to flower
interrupted by my misdeeds

… Thinks my mind, churning
doubts, torn, anxious.

PRATIHĀRĪ: I think the ascetics have come to praise you for your good behaviour.

(*Śārṅgarava, Śāradvata and other ascetics enter, with Gautamī presenting Śakuntalā. They are led by Kañcukī and the priest*)

KAÑCUKĪ: This way, this way.

ŚĀRṄGARAVA: Śāradvata,

Maybe the great king's
on the straight and narrow,
Not even the oppressed castes stray.

Yet this crowded house seems
like a house on fire to my
mind used to solitude.

ŚĀRADVATA: It's natural you've become so, on entering the city. Me too—

As a bathed man sees an oil-smeared man
As a pure man sees an impure one
As a man awake sees a man asleep

As a free man sees a captive

I see these hedonists

ŚAKUNTALĀ: (*Senses an omen*) Uhh, why does my right eye twitch!

GAUTAMĪ: (*Walks around*) Śakuntalā, may negative things be diverted. May your husband's family deities give you joys.

PRIEST: (*Points to the king*) Look, ascetics, here he is, protector of the social order, He's got off his seat, and waits for you.

ŚĀRṄGARAVA: You must be a great brahmin, and all of this is obviously commendable. But we don't care either way. Because …

Trees bow humbly in fruit season
Clouds with fresh water hang low
Good men are unproud at success
That's the nature of the benevolent

PRATIHĀRĪ: King, their faces look happy. I think the ascetics are on a peaceful mission.

DUṢYANTA: (*Sees Śakuntalā*) In that case, what about the lady here?

Who's this

veiled woman,
her body-beauty
not too clear

Amidst ascetics

like a bud amidst
withered leaves

PRATIHĀRĪ: I'm full of curiosity, but my guess doesn't lead anywhere. Her figure calls for a second look.

DUṢYANTA: Enough. One must not look at another man's wife.

ŚAKUNTALĀ: (*Hand on her chest, to herself*) Why do I tremble so? Trust the king's love, and be brave.

PRIEST: (*Goes forward*) These ascetics have been ritually welcomed. There's some message from their teacher. The king has to hear it.

DUṢYANTA: I'm all ears.

ASCETICS: (*Raises their hands to bless*) Greetings!

DUṢYANTA: I welcome you all.

ASCETICS: May your wishes come true.

DUṢYANTA: I hope the ascetics are able to meditate without disturbance?

ASCETICS:

> Where you're the guardian of good people
> There's no hitch in good work
>
> How will darkness show
> when the sun blazes

DUṢYANTA: Now that makes my title 'King' meaningful. And for the benefit of the world, is Sage Kaṇva doing well?

ASCETICS: Advanced yogis have their health under their own control. He asked after your health, and said this…

DUṢYANTA: What does Sage Kaṇva command?

ŚĀRṄGARAVA: 'That you secretly made love to and married my daughter, I permit, with goodwill to both of you. Because:

> We know you're the best
> of the worthy
>
> Śakuntalā, good-deeds
> incarnate

Pairing a bride and groom
of equal merit

Finally the creator
escaped criticism

Take her now as your companion in dharma, she's pregnant.

GAUTAMĪ: King, I want to say something. Though there's no need for my opinion. Because:

She didn't approach elders
You didn't ask the family
In this kind of mutual behaviour—
What to say to either

ŚAKUNTALĀ: (*To herself*) What's he going to say?

DUṢYANTA: What's this lecture!

ŚAKUNTALĀ: Oh calling it 'lecture' is like fire.

ŚĀRṄGARAVA: What 'what'? You know the ways of the world all too well.

When a married woman lives
alone in her family home

People suspect her even if
she's chaste

A woman's family wants her loved,
or unloved, near her husband

DUṢYANTA: And I already married this woman?

ŚAKUNTALĀ: (*Sadly, to herself*) My fears have come true.

ŚĀRṄGARAVA: Is this a hatred, or deliberate disregard, for the done deed? Or a turning away from dharma?

DUṢYANTA: Why this imaginary, false accusation?

ŚĀRṄGARAVA: Such changes usually happen under the intoxicating influence of power.

DUṢYANTA: I'm being seriously put down.

GAUTAMĪ: Śakuntalā, just for a moment, don't be shy. I'll remove your veil. Then your husband will recognize you. (*Does so*)

DUṢYANTA: (*Looks at Śakuntalā. To himself*)

> Offered this way, this beauty
> of unspoiled radiance
>
> Did I marry her
> already, or no?
>
> Wondering …
> Like a bee at dawn
>
> Can't relish or decline
> a dew-filled Kunda flower

(*Thinks, stands*)

PRATIHĀRĪ: Oh how mindful of dharma the king is. Who else will hesitate, looking at such beauty, easily available?

ŚĀRṄGARAVA: Why so silent, King?

DUṢYANTA: Even after thinking, I don't remember marrying this lady here. Then how can I rush towards her, with evident sign of pregnancy, when I don't think I'm the father?

ŚAKUNTALĀ: (*Aside*) The king has doubts even about the marriage. Where's my high-flying desire now?

ŚĀRṄGARAVA: Don't say that.

> The sage allowed your
> groping his daughter

He deserves insult, for
You're honoured

Like a robber asked to keep
the loot as your own

ŚĀRADVATA: Śārṅgarava, now you stop! Śakuntalā, what has to be said has been said by us. And this king here has spoken as he has. Give him a reply with proof.

ŚAKUNTALĀ: (*Aside*) When such a passion has come to this state, what's the point of a reminder? My life's miserable, it's come to pass. (*Aloud*) Husband (*Stops in the middle*)—now that's not the right way to address him when the very marriage is in question. King, it's not fitting of you to deceive an open-hearted person in the āśrama with a promise, and now to deny everything with such words.

DUṢYANTA: (*Closes his ears*) Quiet, evil!

Do you want to spoil my name?
Topple me

Like river Sindhu ravages
its clear water, banks and trees?

ŚAKUNTALĀ: All right. If you are this way because you're really in doubt that I am another's wife, I'll remove your doubt with this souvenir.

DUṢYANTA: A great idea.

ŚAKUNTALĀ: (*Touches her ring finger*) Alas! My finger's without a ring! (*Looks forlorn at Gautamī*)

GAUTAMĪ: For sure the ring slipped when you were worshipping the waters of Śacītīrtha at Śakrāvatāra.

DUṢYANTA: (*With a smile*) This is an example of women's quick-witted brains.

ŚAKUNTALĀ: Fate has shown its power here. I'll tell you something else.

DUṢYANTA: Now this must be heard.

ŚAKUNTALĀ: One day, in the Navamallikā vine bower, you had in your hand, water in a bowl made of lotus leaves.

DUṢYANTA: I'm listening.

ŚAKUNTALĀ: At that moment, the fawn Wide-Eyes, my adopted son, was there. 'He drinks first,' you insisted compassionately, with the water. Not being familiar with you, he didn't come near your hands. Later when the same water was held by me, he loved it. Then you laughed like this—'Everyone trusts their own kind. Both of you are forest-dwellers.'

DUṢYANTA: Hedonists are attracted by such and other sweet, false words of women who achieve their own ends.

GAUTAMĪ: Generous King, you mustn't say so. Brought up in an āśrama, she does not know cunning.

DUṢYANTA: Old ascetic woman,

> Women's cunning's seen
> even in animals, untaught.
> Imagine when trainable.
>
> Before taking off to the skies,
> cuckoos get other birds
> to feed their fledglings.

ŚAKUNTALĀ: (*With anger*) You judge others on the basis of your own nature. No one's like you, dressed in the clothing of dharma, a well hidden by grass.

DUṢYANTA: (*To himself*) Her anger seems genuine, puts my mind in doubt.

When I—
Horrible Forgetful—

We made love in secret

Very red-eyed, she—

Arched eyebrows knitted in anger
Snapped Kāma's bow

(*Aloud*) Good woman, Duṣyanta's actions are well known, but this is not found.

ŚAKUNTALĀ: (*Covers her face in the hem of her shawl and weeps*) I deserve it then. I've been turned into a whore by falling into the hands of this man of the Puru race—poison-hearted honey-mouth.

ŚĀRṄGARAVA: This is how insolent, wilful actions devastate.

Think before you love,
in secret, especially

Friendship turns to enmity
when the hearts are strangers'

DUṢYANTA: Why do you hurt me with abusive words just on the basis of what this woman swears?

ŚĀRṄGARAVA: (*Sarcastically*) You misunderstood me.

The man who from birth
never learned deceit

his words,
unbelievable

And he who is learned
in fooling others

Yes, let his words
be veda

DUṢYANTA: Oh Truth-teller, all this is fine by me. But what do I get by deceiving her?

ŚĀRṄGARAVA: Downfall!

DUṢYANTA: Those of the Puru race seeking downfall? Absurd.

ŚĀRADVATA: Śārṅgarava, what do you gain by answering him? We've done our teacher's errand. (*To the king*)

This is your wife
Love her or leave her

That's right. Husbands' rights
over wives are total

Gautamī, lead.

(*They begin to leave*)

ŚAKUNTALĀ: How I've been deceived by this cheat. You too abandon me even as I'm weeping!

GAUTAMĪ: Śārṅgarava, Śakuntalā follows us weeping miserably. What can my daughter do, when so harshly rejected by her husband?

ŚĀRṄGARAVA: (*Turns angrily*) Wretched woman, would you dare be rebellious?

(*A frightened Śakuntalā trembles*)

ŚĀRṄGARAVA: Śakuntalā—

You are what the king says you are.
What's Father got to do with you?—

You're a slur to family honour.
If you think you're chaste

It's okay even to be a servant
in your husband's home

Stay. We go.

DUṢYANTA: Ascetic! Do you reject her?

The sun wakes only lotuses
The moon, only water-lilies

Yogis avoid hanging out
with others' wives

ŚĀRṄGARAVA: How can you—who has forgotten what you've done because you're now with another woman—how can you be afraid of bad conduct?

DUṢYANTA: (*To the priest*) I ask you what's better, and what's worse.

Am I stupid?
Is she lying?

Unsure—
Should I be

A wife-deserter?
Or foul wife-snatcher?

PRIEST: (*Thoughtfully*) In that case, how about doing this…

DUṢYANTA: Advise me.

PRIEST: Let this lady here stay in my house until her delivery. In case you're wondering why … you've been advised by ascetics that your very first son will be an emperor. If Sage Kaṇva's grandson has such marks, of an emperor, then you'll honour her and take her in. If on the contrary, sending her to her father's side is the only way.

DUṢYANTA: As the Guru wishes.

PRIEST: (*To Śakuntalā*) Follow me.

ŚAKUNTALĀ: Goddess Earth, give me a hole to hide in. (*Crying, makes her way out with the priest and ascetics*)

(*The king, memory obscured by the curse, muses over what happened with Śakuntalā*)

VOICE BACKSTAGE: Amazing!

DUṢYANTA: (*Listens*) What can it be?

(*Priest enters*)

PRIEST: (*Bewildered*) King, something wonderful happened.

DUṢYANTA: Like what?

PRIEST: King, when Kaṇva's disciples left:

> That girl, cursing her fate
> Raising her arms, wailing …

DUṢYANTA: And?

PRIEST:

> All of a sudden near Apsaratīrtha
> *The sacred bathing place of apsarās*
> A light in the shape of a woman
> Lifted her and left

(*Everyone's surprised*)

DUṢYANTA: Sir, I've already rejected her. Why worry with pointless questions? Take it easy.

PRIEST: (*Scrutinizes*) Fine. Be successful!

DUṢYANTA: Vetravatī, I'm disturbed. Show me the way to the bedroom.

VETRAVATĪ: This way, this way, King. (*Begins to leave*)

DUṢYANTA:

I really don't remember taking as wife
the sage's daughter I rejected

But, my heart, so sore
It seems to nag me

END OF ACT V

ACT VI

(*The king's Police Officer enters, followed by two policemen, Sūcaka and Jānuka, escorting a fisherman*)

SŪCAKA AND JĀNUKA: (*They beat the fisherman*) You thief, say where you got hold of this ring with the king's name engraved on it.

FISHERMAN: (*Scared*) Easy, I'm not that kind of man.

SŪCAKA: Oh? Was it given as a gift by the king, thinking of you as some great brahmin?

FISHERMAN: Listen now. I'm a fisherman living near the sacred place Śakrāvatāra.

JĀNUKA: Rogue, were you asked about your profession?

POLICE OFFICER: Sūcaka, let him tell the whole story in the right order. Don't stop him in the middle.

SŪCAKA AND JĀNUKA: As you say, you're the king's brother-in-law. Speak, thief.

FISHERMAN: I support my family by using things that catch fish such as hooks and nets.

POLICE OFFICER: (*Laughs sarcastically*) A lily-white profession!

FISHERMAN:

> The job that's despicable—
> If your dharma is your birthright
> Don't give it up
>
> A priest—ruthless slaughterer
> of a sacrificial animal, in fact
> he's tender with compassion

POLICE OFFICER: Yes, yes, go on.

FISHERMAN: One day, as I was chopping a Rohita fish, I saw this ring, shiny with gems. After that, as I was showing it—for selling it—you caught me. Kill me, or release me. This is the story of how I got it.

POLICE OFFICER: Jānuka, for sure this smelly crocodile-eater is a fisherman. How he found the ring must be considered. Let's go straight to the palace.

SŪCAKA AND JĀNUKA: Okay. Go on, you pickpocket!

(*All walk around*)

POLICE OFFICER: Sūcaka, guard him well at the city gate. Meanwhile, I'll inform the king how we got this ring, get his orders and be back.

SŪCAKA AND JĀNUKA: We hope the king's pleased when you go in.

(*Police Officer leaves*)

SŪCAKA: Jānuka, brother-in-law's late.

JĀNUKA: Kings must be approached at the right moment.

SŪCAKA: My hands long to cover him with a wreath of flowers. (*Points to the fisherman*)

FISHERMAN: The thought of an unjustified murder is unworthy of you.

JĀNUKA: Here's our boss, a paper in hand, coming this way. It seems he has received the king's order. You'll either be the offering to a vulture, or see the face of Death.

(*Police Officer enters*)

POLICE OFFICER: Sūcaka, let this fisherman be freed. It's a fact, how he got the ring.

SŪCAKA: As the king's brother-in-law says.

JĀNUKA: He entered the house of Death and came back! (*Unties the man*)

FISHERMAN: (*Bows with folded hands before the Police Officer*) What about my livelihood now?

POLICE OFFICER: (*Gives the fisherman some money*) Here, a present given by the king, equal to the ring's value.

FISHERMAN: (*Takes it respectfully*) Sir, I'm blessed.

SŪCAKA: Taken down from a stake and hoisted on an elephant! What can you call it but a blessing!

JĀNUKA: The gift suggests—the king must be happy with the ring.

POLICE OFFICER: I think it's not because of the very valuable gem there that the king values it. By seeing it, the king remembered someone he values. Although calm by nature, for a moment he was teary-eyed.

SŪCAKA: That's what one calls well-done, brother-in-law!

JĀNUKA: (*Looks jealously at the fisherman*) By that, he's the king of fishermen!

FISHERMAN: Guard, let half of this be the cost of your wreath!

JĀNUKA: That's right.

POLICE OFFICER: Now that you're more worthy, you've become my dear friend. Our friendship calls for a drink first. We'll go to a bar.

(*They all leave*)

INTRODUCTORY SCENE ENDS

(*Sānumatī, an apsarā, enters by air*)

SĀNUMATĪ: (*Gets off the vehicle*)

I've done my turn minding the holy baths of Apsaratīrtha. While the ascetics bathe, I'll take a look at what the king is up to. My relationship with Menakā has made Śakuntalā a part of me. And I've already been asked to do this for her daughter's sake. (*Looks around*) Why does the royal house look like it hasn't begun any celebrations despite the festive season? Of course, I can know everything by my powers of concentration, but I must be mindful of my friend's trust. Well. I'll stay beside these two girls looking after the garden, hidden by my magic cape, and find out.

(*Looking at mango-blossoms, two maidservants, Parabhṛtikā and Madhukarikā, enter*)

Redgreenyellowish mango-blossom,
You're out—

An invocation of the season

The very soul of the month
of spring

I favour you

MADHUKARIKĀ: Parabhṛtikā, what are you muttering alone?

PARABHṚTIKĀ: Madhukarikā, Parabhṛtikā is besotted just by looking at the mango-blossom.

MADHUKARIKĀ: (*Comes closer in a hurry, happily*) What! Is Spring, the bee season, here?

PARABHṚTIKĀ: Madhukarikā, this is your call for ecstatic, amorous singing.

MADHUKARIKĀ: Parabhṛtikā, hold me so I can stand on my toes, pluck the mango-blossom and pay homage to Kāma.

PARABHṚTIKĀ: Yes, if I can get half the benefit of your homage!

MADHUKARIKĀ: (*Stands supported by her friend, plucks a mango-blossom*) That goes without saying! Our hearts are one, though the body remains split into two. Hmm … although the mango-blossom is not yet fully open, there's a nice fragrance from the snapped stalk!

(*Cups her hands*)

Mango-blossom, you are

My gift to Kāma who's
ready with a bow

Be arrow—

Over and above the five *flowers*
Aimed at young women

who are travellers' lovers

to be struck only
to be bereft

(*Tosses the mango-blossom as if offering to Kāma*)

(*Flinging aside the stage curtain angrily, the chamberlain Kañcukī enters*)

KAÑCUKĪ: Don't do that. Fool, why are you starting to pluck a mango-blossom when the king has forbidden the spring festival?

PARABHṚTIKĀ AND MADHUKARIKĀ: (*Scared*) Please, Sir. We didn't know what it meant.

KAÑCUKĪ: Didn't you both hear? Even the spring-trees and the creatures that live in them have sworn by the king's order …

Mango buds came a while ago
Not their pollen

Ready the Kurabaka remains
in the state of a bud

Winter's gone, but
the male cuckoo's coo
falters in the throat

Afraid, timid Kāma holds back
an arrow half out of the quiver

PARABHṚTIKĀ AND MADHUKARIKĀ: Without doubt, a very powerful king.

PARABHṚTIKĀ: We were sent some days back by the king's brother-in-law Mitrāvasu, to the Queen Mother's service. So we were given the job of looking after the pleasure garden. Having just come, we hadn't heard this news.

KAÑCUKĪ: Okay. You mustn't do so again.

PARABHṚTIKĀ AND MADHUKARIKĀ: Sir, we're curious. If it's fine to be heard by another person, do tell. Why did the king ban the spring festival?

SĀNUMATĪ: Human beings are fond of festivals. There must be an important reason.

KAÑCUKĪ: Why can't I say when it's common knowledge? Has it not come to your ears, the scandal about sending away Śakuntalā?

PARABHṚTIKĀ AND MADHUKARIKĀ: We've heard from the king's brother-in-law's mouth about what happened up until the seeing of the ring.

KAÑCUKĪ: Then very little needs to be said. On seeing his ring, the king remembered—'Indeed, I married that lady Śakuntalā in secret, and sent her away out of confusion.' From that very moment, the king was regretful. That's why:

Dislike
for what's likeable

Unavailable to ministers every day
like he used to before

Spends nights awake
rolling about the bed

Speaks only from politeness
to his queens at home

Forgetting their names, he's embarrassed,
mortified for a while

SĀNUMATĪ: Serves him right!

KAÑCUKĪ: The festival is banned because of his sad state.

PARABHṚTIKĀ AND MADHUKARIKĀ: Makes sense.

VOICE BACKSTAGE: This way, this way, Sir.

KAÑCUKĪ: (*Listens*) The king's coming right here. Go about your business.

PARABHṚTIKĀ AND MADHUKARIKĀ: Okay.

(*The king enters wearing clothes to suit his remorse, along with Mādhavya and attendant Vetravatī*)

KAÑCUKĪ: (*Looks at the king*) Special people look good under all circumstances. The king looks good although he's so worried.

Declined choice costumes and jewelleries
Except a gold bracelet on his left wrist, loose

Anxious, amnesiac eyes hollow
Breath-baked lips bloodless

Like a great diamond ground on a stone,
Thanks to inner radiance

Doesn't look worn

SĀNUMATĪ: (*Looks at the king*) No wonder Śakuntalā pines for his sake, though insulted and sent away.

DUṢYANTA: (*Walks slowly, pensive*)

> Asleep even when roused by beloved deer-eyes
> This cursed heart
> Now wide awake for sad regret

SĀNUMATĪ: The poor girl's fate, this.

MĀDHAVYA: (*Aside*) Crippled again! By the disease called Śakuntalā. Don't know how he must be cured.

KAÑCUKĪ: King, I've inspected the pleasure-garden grounds. The king may sit in any delightful place, wherever he wishes.

DUṢYANTA: Vetravatī, talk to Minister Piśuna on my behalf. As I was awake for too long, I'm unable to preside over the courts today. Whatever he has decided about public issues, write it down in a letter and send it.

VETRAVATĪ: As the king commands. (*She leaves*)

DUṢYANTA: Kañcukī, you too carry on with the rest of your work.

KAÑCUKĪ: As the king commands. (*Leaves*)

MĀDHAVYA: You've made it so there's not even a fly here! Now you'll amuse yourself in this pleasure garden shaded from the season's heat.

DUṢYANTA: There's no exception to the saying that 'disasters fall upon us all at once when there's an opening'.

> My mind's now free
> of dullness masking my
> memory of making love
> with the sage's daughter
>
> But mind-born Kāma
> keen to strike
> fixed to his bow
> a mango-blossom arrow

MĀDHAVYA: Hold it, then. I'll smash the disease of Kāma's arrow with this stick. (*Beats the mango-blossoms with a stick*)

DUṢYANTA: (*With a smile*) Let it be. Your power as a brahmin is evident. Sitting here, I am enjoying the view of vines that somewhat resemble my sweetheart's figure.

MĀDHAVYA: Didn't you send the assistant Caturikā to fetch it? You said, 'I'll spend this time in the bower of the Mādhavī vine—the painting drawn by my own hand of Śakuntalā's image—bring it there.'

DUṢYANTA: That's a spot that entertains my heart. Then show me that path.

MĀDHAVYA: This way, this way, Sir.

(*Both walk about, Sānumatī follows*)

MĀDHAVYA: Here's the Mādhavī bower with a marble slab expecting us as if, no doubt, with a nice, welcoming gift.

(*Both enter and sit*)

SĀNUMATĪ: I'll lean on the vines and see my friend's portrait. (*Does so*) Then I'll let her know her husband's great passion for her.

DUṢYANTA: Now I remember every previous event related to Śakuntalā. (*To Mādhavya*) I told you too. You weren't near me when I sent her away. You never even mentioned her name to me before. You're as forgetful as me.

MĀDHAVYA: I don't forget. But after narrating everything, you said it's 'not so, just babbling for fun'. And I—muddle-headed that I am—I took it that way. Or, what's meant to be is powerful.

SĀNUMATĪ: So it is.

DUṢYANTA: (*Thinks*) Help me, friend.

MĀDHAVYA: What about? This doesn't suit you! Noble people are never affected by grief. And mountains don't shake in the wind.

DUṢYANTA: I feel very lost when I think of my sweetheart's state of bewilderment when rejected.

> Sent away from here she tried
> to follow her family
>
> 'STAY'—said her father's disciple
> —he was father-like
>
> Thick tears flowing
> She looked again at me, cruel me
>
> That look burns me
> Like a poison-tipped arrow

SĀNUMATĪ: So much selfishness, eh! I enjoy this remorse.

MĀDHAVYA: Hey, I wonder … the lady must have been taken away by some celestial.

DUṢYANTA: Who's interested in touching a woman who worships her husband as god? I heard Śakuntalā's mother is Menakā. My heart suspects her mother's friends carried her away.

SĀNUMATĪ: His confusion is amusing, not his return to consciousness!

MĀDHAVYA: If that's the case, then you'll meet her in due course.

DUṢYANTA: How so?

MĀDHAVYA: Parents wouldn't bear the sight of their daughter saddened by separation from her husband.

DUṢYANTA:

> Dream—illusion—imagination—or
> leftover of past merit?
>
> It's gone
> Beyond to
> Never return

Hopes, rocks on slopes
Meant to crumble

MĀDHAVYA: Don't say that. Just the recovery of the ring is a sure indication that there will be a reunion.

DUṢYANTA: (*Looks at the ring*) I'm sorry for this, which slipped from a place that's hard to get.

Ring, the outcome shows
your merits slim, like mine

You made it to those fingers
Nails the colour of bewitching dawn

And fell

SĀNUMATĪ: Had it gone to some other hand, truly, that would be regrettable.

MĀDHAVYA: Why did our lady there receive this ring with your name?

SĀNUMATĪ: He expresses my own curiosity.

DUṢYANTA: Listen. When I left for my city, a tearful Śakuntalā asked me, 'How long will it take for you to send me an acknowledgement?'

MĀDHAVYA: And then?

DUṢYANTA: Then, putting this ring on her finger, I said:

Count the letters of my name
one by one, each day, to the end

Then, my love, the people
who will lead you to

a formal entrance to
the queens' section of my house

will come to you

And I did not follow through because of my delusion.

SĀNUMATĪ: A nice idea, flouted by fate.

MĀDHAVYA: Then, how was it in the belly of the Rohita fish caught by the fisherman?

DUṢYANTA: When Śakuntalā prayed at Śacītīrtha, it slipped from her hand into the waters of river Gaṅgā.

MĀDHAVYA: That's possible.

SĀNUMATĪ: And is that why the king, so mindful of not being dhārmic, doubted his marriage with poor Śakuntalā? On the other hand, does love of this sort need a souvenir? How's that so?

DUṢYANTA: So I'll scold this ring.

MĀDHAVYA: (*To himself*) He's gone way crazy.

DUṢYANTA:

> Why did you leave
> that hand of delicate fingers
> and sink in water?
>
> An inanimate thing
> can't recognize virtue
>
> But why was she rejected
> by me *evidently animate*?

MĀDHAVYA: (*To himself*) Wonder why I'm ravished by hunger?

DUṢYANTA: Pity me with a vision of you, me—whose heart is racked with regret for needlessly abandoning you…

(*Attendant Caturikā enters with a toss of the curtain, carrying a canvas-board in her hand*)

CATURIKĀ: (*Shows the canvas-board*) Here she is, in a picture.

MĀDHAVYA: Great. A sweet picture, worth seeing—full of feeling. My sight trips on the elevations and depths.

SĀNUMATĪ: This is the king's talent. I feel as if my friend is before me.

DUṢYANTA:

> What's no good in the picture
> All that's revised
>
> Yet the lines barely
> Capture her beauty

SĀNUMATĪ: Spoken like someone whose love's deeper with regret and humility.

MĀDHAVYA: Hmm … there are three ladies there. All pretty. Which one of them is Śakuntalā?

SĀNUMATĪ: About such beauty, this fellow's ignorant. His eyes, useless.

DUṢYANTA: Who do you think?

MĀDHAVYA: I guess she—hair-knot loose—flowers dropping from her hair—drops of sweat risen on her face—arms drooping, especially—beside the mango tree—watered—new leaves, shiny—drawn as if tired—she's Śakuntalā. The other two, her friends.

DUṢYANTA: You're good! It's a picture of my feelings.

> At the borders of the painting
> See my sweaty fingerprints
>
> See here—the colour's off where
> My tears fell on her cheek

Caturikā, this painting I enjoy is only half-done. Go fetch my brush.

CATURIKĀ: Mādhavya, hold the canvas-board till I come back.

DUṢYANTA: I'll hold it myself. (*Does so*)

(*Caturikā leaves*)

DUṢYANTA: (*Sighs*)

> My lover came to me
> She herself
>
> I spurned her then
> Make much
> of her image now
>
> My friend,
>
> I crossed a river flowing
> with ample water en route
>
> Long for a mirage now

MĀDHAVYA: (*To himself*) Okay, so our man here has crossed a river and gone to a mirage. (*Aloud*) What else needs to be drawn here?

SĀNUMATĪ: He might want to draw places that my friend likes.

DUṢYANTA: Listen.

> I want to create
>
> By the flowing river Mālinī
> A swan-pair lying on the sand
>
> Around them the foothills
> of sacred Himālaya
>
> Deer sitting under a tree
> where bark-garments hang
>
> Rubbing her left eye on a black deer's horn,
> a doe

MĀDHAVYA: As I see it, the canvas has to be filled with heaps of long-beard sadhus.

DUṢYANTA: One more thing. I forgot the jewellery meant for Śakuntalā.

MĀDHAVYA: Like what?

DUṢYANTA: Something suitable for someone simple and delicate who lives in a forest.

> I haven't drawn the Śirīṣa flower ear-ring
> its stamens lolling
> on her cheek
>
> Nor the soft light of the winter moon
> in her cleavage
> Lotus-fibre-like

MĀDHAVYA: Why does the lady there stand confused—bewildered—covering her face with her palm, which is red as a lotus petal? Argh it's this whoreson nectar-thief bee lunging at her face.

DUṢYANTA: Then stop the cheeky fellow.

MĀDHAVYA: Only you, the punisher of the shameless, will be able to ward it off.

DUṢYANTA: Right. Hey dear guest of flowers and vines. Why so obsessive, whirling around her?

> Smitten by you this
> female bee sits
>
> in a flower thirsty
> yet waits, won't
>
> sip nectar
> without you

SĀNUMATĪ: Now he's been warded off politely.

MĀDHAVYA: This species is perverse, even when forbidden.

DUṢYANTA: Oh? You won't stop at my order! Then listen now:

> If, bee, you dare touch
> my love's Bimba-fruit-red lower lip
> Desirable as an untouched leaf of a young tree
> Even in love-fests I only sipped it tenderly
> I'll jail you in the belly of a lotus

MĀDHAVYA: (*Laughs, to himself*) How come he's not scared of such severe punishment! Mad, then. In his company, I've also become like that. (*Aloud*) It's only a picture.

DUṢYANTA: What do you mean, picture?

SĀNUMATĪ: I didn't understand that either! How could he—who's going through what's in the picture?

DUṢYANTA: Why did you do this terrible thing.

> I was rapt
> Enjoying the sight
> —as if real—
>
> You've made me remember
> Turned my lover into an image again

(*Cries*)

SĀNUMATĪ: The style of this separation … contrary then, and contrary now.

DUṢYANTA: How's it that I feel sad, without pause?

> Loving her, if only in a dream—
> Waking interrupts

Seeing her, if only in a painting
Tears get in the way

SĀNUMATĪ: You've made up for all of Śakuntalā's grief at rejection.

(*Caturikā enters*)

CATURIKĀ: King! I was coming this way with the box of brushes.

DUṢYANTA: And?

CATURIKĀ: Queen Vasumatī—attended by Taralikā—snatched it forcibly from my hand, saying, 'I'll take it to him myself.'

MĀDHAVYA: Lucky you were released!

CATURIKĀ: As Taralikā was disentangling the queen's shawl that was caught in a tree, I escaped!

DUṢYANTA: Mādhavya, the queen's here, she takes pride in how she's treated. Keep this image safe.

MĀDHAVYA: You can say that about yourself! (*Takes the painting, gets up*) If you ever escape from domestic intrigues, call for me, at the Meghapraticchanda Mansion. (*Leaves in a hurry, with quick steps*)

SĀNUMATĪ: Though his heart has moved on to another, he treats his first wife with regard—he's been rather slack in his affections lately.

(*Vetravatī enters, with a letter in hand*)

VETRAVATĪ: Jai, Jai, King!

DUṢYANTA: Vetravatī, did you see the queen on the way?

VETRAVATĪ: What if? Seeing me with a letter in hand, she went back.

DUṢYANTA: She understands the importance of duty, avoids disturbing my work.

VETRAVATĪ: King, the Minister says: 'Busy counting large revenues, only one civic affair was handled. That's been put on paper, please look into it.'

DUṢYANTA: Show me the paper.

(*Vetravatī takes it out*)

DUṢYANTA: (*Reads*) What—a sea-merchant named Dhanamitra killed in a shipwreck. No children, a sad man. His assets go to the king—so writes the Minister. Tough having no children. Being very rich, he surely has many wives. Enquire if any of his wives are pregnant.

VETRAVATĪ: King, the latest news is that his wife, the daughter of a merchant from Sāketa, had the ritual celebration of her pregnancy.

DUṢYANTA: Then the child in the womb gets the paternal inheritance. Go. Tell that to the Minister.

VETRAVATĪ: As you say, King. (*Starts to leave*)

DUṢYANTA: Come here!

VETRAVATĪ: Here I am.

DUṢYANTA: Child, no child, why does it matter.

Announce:

> Whosoever has lost
> close kin—except for
> illicit relationships—
>
> Duṣyanta's theirs

VETRAVATĪ: It will be announced. (*Leaves, re-enters*) The king's decree was welcomed like timely rain.

DUṢYANTA: (*A hot and deep sigh*) Yes it's like that. Without children to depend on, assets of families pass on to a stranger when the head of the family dies. When I die, the fortunes of the Puru race will also be like that. Like a land in which a seed is planted at the wrong time.

VETRAVATĪ: Hope such a disaster is prevented!

DUṢYANTA: Hell. It's my fault. Insulted the luck that was right there.

SĀNUMATĪ: For sure, it's with my friend in mind that he berates himself.

DUṢYANTA:

I impregnated my wife
Like sowing the earth

At the right time
For great results

She whom I abandoned, actually, is
the foundation of my race.

SĀNUMATĪ: Now your lineage will not be interrupted.

CATURIKĀ: (*To Vetravatī*) With this news about the sea-merchant, the king's agony is doubled. Catch hold of Mādhavya from the Meghapraticchanda Mansion to console him, and return.

VETRAVATĪ: Good idea. (*Leaves*)

DUṢYANTA: The spirits of Duṣyanta's ancestors stir with doubts.

My ancestral spirits drink
what's left

after I—childless I—
wash my tears

They think,

Who after me,
who in the race

will make ritual
offerings?

(*Faints*)

CATURIKĀ: (*Looks confused*) Take it easy, King!

SĀNUMATĪ: Oh! Oh! There's light, but he experiences darkness because of the screen. I'll make him happy right away. But wait. I heard from the mouth of Indra's mother who was consoling Śakuntalā … the gods, eager to enjoy the offerings at rituals, will make it so that he will welcome his wife soon. So it's better to wait out this time. Meanwhile, I'll console Śakuntalā with this news. (*Flies up, leaves*)

MĀDHAVYA BACKSTAGE: Good heavens! Help! Brahmin-under-attack!

DUṢYANTA: (*Revives, listens*) That vexed cry is Mādhavya's. Who's there?

(*Attendant Pratihārī enters*)

PRATIHĀRĪ: (*Agitated*) King, save a friend in trouble.

DUṢYANTA: The basket-case rattled? By whom?

PRATIHĀRĪ: He was overpowered and put on the roof of the Meghapraticchanda Mansion by some invisible spirit.

DUṢYANTA: (*Gets up*) No! My house won't be taken over by spirits!

Impossible to know from day to day
one's own foolish mistakes

Where's the energy
to figure out the rest—

among my people

Who does how?

MĀDHAVYA BACKSTAGE: Help! Help! My friend! Friend! No way!

DUṢYANTA: (*Rushes around*) Hey my friend, don't be afraid, don't be afraid!

MĀDHAVYA BACKSTAGE (*In the same vein*) How can I not fear? Someone breaks me into three pieces, my back is bent like the stem of a sugarcane.

DUṢYANTA: (*Casts a glance*) My bow, then.

(*Attendant Yavani enters with bow in hand*)

YAVANI: King, here's the bow, along with the armguard.

(*The king takes the bow with arrow and armguard*)

VOICE BACKSTAGE:

Like a tiger hungry
for fresh blood

at the neck of an animal
in its last throes

I'll kill you

Now armed with a bow
to take away the fear

of the oppressed
Duṣyanta's your end-all

DUṢYANTA: (*Angrily*) This implicates me. Hold it, you corpse-eater! You will no longer be! (*Strings the bow*) Yavani show the way to the stairs.

YAVANI: This way, King, this way.

(*Everyone leaves in a hurry*)

DUṢYANTA: (*Looks all around*) There's nothing here.

MĀDHAVYA BACKSTAGE: Help! Help! I see you here. You don't see me. Like a mouse caught by a cat, I'm desperate for my life.

DUṢYANTA: Hey you, are you arrogant about your power to be invisible? My weapon sees you. I'm fixing that kind of arrow.

> Will kill you who
> must be killed
>
> Save the brahmin
> who must be saved
>
> In a milk-water mix
> A swan can
>
> Discard the water
> Drink the milk

(*Fixes the arrow*)

(*Mātali enters*)

MĀTALI:

> On friends, good people cast
> mild and genial glances
> Not dreadful arrows
>
> Indra's made the demons your targets
> So draw your bow on them

DUṢYANTA: (*Restrains the arrow*) Ah it's Mātali, Indra's charioteer, welcome!

(*Mādhavya enters*)

MĀDHAVYA: He who treated me like a sacrificial animal, now greeted with a welcome!

MĀTALI: (*With a smile*) King, hear why Indra sent me to you.

DUṢYANTA: I'm attentive.

MĀTALI: There's a band of demons called Durjaya, Kālanemi's children.

DUṢYANTA: Yes. I've heard of them from Nārada.

MĀTALI:

> That group's unbeatable even by
> your hundred-strong friend, Indra
>
> At the battlefront you're called
> its destroyer
>
> The moon dispels the darkness
> that the seven-horsed sun cannot

DUṢYANTA: I'm favoured by this idea of Indra's. But then why did you behave like that towards Mādhavya?

MĀTALI: I'll explain that too. I saw that you're disturbed, for some reason, from some emotional upset. I behaved like that to anger you.

> When embers are stirred, fire blazes
> A provoked serpent opens its hood
>
> It's when they're angered that
> people usually regain power

DUṢYANTA: (*To Mādhavya*) The command of the chief of gods cannot be disobeyed. So make sense of what happened here, and tell Minister Piśuna on my behalf:

> Let only your wisdom
> look after the people
>
> This strung bow's busy
> On another job

MĀDHAVYA: As the king says. (*Leaves*)

MĀTALI: Get into the chariot, King.

(*The king mimes climbing into a chariot*)

(*Everyone leaves*)

END OF ACT VI

ACT VII

(*The king and Mātali enter by air*)

DUṢYANTA: Mātali, I've done what Indra said. But I feel I've not been as useful as the special reception suggests.

MĀTALI: (*Smiles*) Both of you feel dissatisfied.

> You think little
> of the favour you did Indra
> compared to his gifts
>
> And amazed at your heroic acts
> He doesn't count the extent
> of the honours

DUṢYANTA: Not so, Mātali. The honours at the farewell were way out of line with what anyone could desire. Me, near the gods, seated on half his throne …

> Indra garlanded me while he
> looked up at Jayanta with a smile
>
> The garland of Mandāra flowers
> was marked with saffron sandal-paste
> rubbed off his own chest
>
> Jayanta right beside me,
> jealous

MĀTALI: Don't you, the king, deserve this honour from Indra, chief of the gods?

> Twice the thorn of demons
> removed

from fun-loving Indra's
heaven

Then by the nails
of Narasimhā
Viṣṇu's incarnation

Now by your smooth-jointed
arrows

DUṢYANTA: But it is Indra's greatness that must be praised here.

When workers achieve great things
The credit goes to their boss

Realize that
If the thousand-rayed *Sun*
had not placed

Aruṇa *charioteer*
at the front

he would not be
the Terror of darkness

MĀTALI: That's nice of you. (*Goes a little ahead*) See from here, your fame and good fortune, written on the walls of heaven.

Composing poems
that can be sung

Those who live in heaven
write your exploits

on leaf garments from wish-fulfilling trees
with cosmetic colour pencils
of celestial beauties

DUṢYANTA: When we came up yesterday, I was so excited fighting demons that I did not notice the road to heaven. What wind-path are we on [*of the seven wind-paths to heaven*]?

MĀTALI:

They call this the path
of wind Parivaha

Free of darkness
The second stride of Viṣṇu

Along that river of three streams
located in heaven—
Gaṅgā, who

Propels celestial bodies
Scatters their light

See the story of Bali for
Viṣṇu's second step
as Vāmana

DUṢYANTA: No wonder my outer and inner senses are elated. (*Looks at a part of the chariot*) We've descended to the path of the clouds.

MĀTALI: How do you know?

DUṢYANTA:

Rim moist with spray

In the interstices of spokes,
Cātaka-bird flights and

horses tinted
in lightning flashes

It's your chariot that betrays the route
Over rain-bearing clouds

MĀTALI: In seconds you will be in the land you rule.

DUṢYANTA: (*Looks down*) Because of the speedy descent, the world of people is an astonishing sight.

> As if the Earth descends
> from high-peaked hills
>
> Trees lost in leaves emerge
> as trunks become visible
>
> Thinness gone, expanding,
> rivers assert themselves
>
> As if the Earth is flung up
> by someone
>
> Brought to my side

MĀTALI: Well spotted. (*Looks dutifully*) Yes, the Earth is vast and pleasing.

DUṢYANTA: What's this mountain, plunged into the eastern and western seas, oozing a golden liquid—it looks like a wall of evening clouds.

MĀTALI: This is the mountain Hemakūṭa, the mountain of demi-gods, the place where one can achieve yogic powers.

> Prajāpati, Kaśyapa
> born from
>
> Marīci the father
> of the gods
>
> Meditates there
> with his wife

DUṢYANTA: Then good things must not be overlooked. I'd like to proceed only after circumambulating him.

MĀTALI: A first-class idea.

(*They climb down*)

DUṢYANTA: (*Amazed*)

Reins not drawn in
No ground contact

The chariot   Rims soundless
No dust visible

Although descended
Does not seem so

MĀTALI: That's the only difference between Indra and you!

DUṢYANTA: Where is Kaśyapa's āśrama?

MĀTALI: (*Points with his hand*)

There stands the sage
Facing the sun
Still as a hill

Wears a shoulder-length mesh of hair
where Śakunta birds nest

Throat pressed by a ring
of thick old vine

A figure half
buried in an anthill

Chest covered
in snakeskins

DUṢYANTA: Namaste to a hard-working yogi.

MĀTALI: (*Draws in the reins of the chariot*) King, we have arrived at the āśrama of Prajāpati, where Mandāra trees are nurtured by Aditi, mother of the gods.

DUṢYANTA: It's better than heaven! I'm submerged, like in a pool of nectar.

MĀTALI: (*Stops the chariot*) Do get off.

DUṢYANTA: (*Gets off*) How about you?

MĀTALI: I've stopped the chariot. I'll get off too. See the āśrama grounds of the sages.

DUṢYANTA: Yes, I'm looking with wonder.

> In this forest of wish-fulfilling trees
> They live on air
>
> In waters yellow with the pollen of golden lotuses
> Ritual ablutions
>
> On gem-studded stone-slabs
> Meditation
>
> In the presence of apsarās
> Self-control
>
> A place other sages want to get to
> by penance

MĀTALI: Great people aim high.

(*Walks around in the sky*)

Hey Vṛddhaśākalya, what keeps Kaśyapa busy? What did you say? As requested by Aditi, he is speaking with the wives of great sages about the dharma of a good wife.

DUṢYANTA: (*Listens*) We must wait for the sages.

MĀTALI: (*Looks at the king*) You be under this Aśoka tree, meanwhile I'll look for a chance to announce you to Indra's father, Sage Kaśyapa.

DUṢYANTA: As you see fit.

MĀTALI: I'll go. (*Leaves*)

DUṢYANTA: (*Senses an omen*)

> I don't hope for
> my desire *Śakuntalā*
>
> Then hey, arm, why
> throb in vain?
> *A bad omen*
>
> Spurned fortune
> turns into misfortune

VOICE BACKSTAGE: Don't be naughty. What, have you gone back to your natural state?

DUṢYANTA: (*Listens*) This isn't the place for rudeness. Who's being scolded? (*Looks in the direction of the voice*) Who's this boy, quite unlike a boy, minded by two women ascetics?

> Forcibly drags to play
> A lion-cub
>
> Half-suckled at his mother's breasts
> Hair tangled, handled rough

(*Sarvadamana enters, as described, with two ascetic women*)

DUṢYANTA: (*Listens*)

SARVADAMANA: Open your mouth, Lion. I'll count your teeth.

FIRST WOMAN: Rude boy! Why mess with creatures we've raised no different from our own children? You're growing wilder. It's appropriate that the sages named you Sarvadamana, tamer-of-all.

DUṢYANTA: Why does my heart like this boy, as if he's a son of my own flesh and blood? Childlessness makes me feel parental.

SECOND WOMAN: Here's the lioness that will leap at you if you don't release her child.

SARVADAMANA: (*With a teasing smile*) Oooh, I'm sooo scared!

DUṢYANTA:

> Seems to me
> this boy's the seed of
> someone very powerful
>
> Like fire waiting
> for fuel

FIRST WOMAN: My dear, release this lion-cub. Then I'll give you a toy.

SARVADAMANA: (*Stretches his hand*) Where? Give it to me.

DUṢYANTA: What! He even has the marks of an Emperor.

> Eagerly stretched towards
> a desired object
>
> The hand shows
> close-knit fingers
>
> Like a lotus blown open
> by new dawn
>
> Interstices between petals
> invisible, lit red

SECOND WOMAN: Suvratā, it's not possible to control him with just words. You go. In my hut there's the coloured clay peacock of Sage Mārkaṇḍeya's son. Give it to him.

FIRST WOMAN: Sure. (*Leaves*)

SARVADAMANA: Meanwhile I'll play only with this lion-cub. (*Looks at the ascetic woman, laughs*)

DUṢYANTA: I do like this cheeky boy.

> Lucky those who carry
> their kids—comfy-lap lovers
>
> Who get nice and dirty
> with their muddy limbs
>
> In their for-no-reason laughs
> Spot the cute teeth-buds
>
> Words-letters jumbled
> The babble's adorable

SECOND WOMAN: Okay, he doesn't listen to me. (*Looks around*) Who's there among the sages' sons? (*Sees the king*) You look like a good man, come here. Release this lion-cub held by this tight grip, it's being pestered in a stupid game.

DUṢYANTA: (*Approaches, smiling*) Hey, son of a great sage:

> Self-restraint's in
> your very origins
>
> Then why this attitude
> Contrary to the āśrama
>
> You spoil the happy home
> of animals
>
> Like a young black serpent
> on a sandalwood tree

SECOND WOMAN: Sir, he is not the son of a sage.

DUṢYANTA: His looks and behaviour also suggest that. I thought as I did because of the location.

(*Doing as requested, he goes towards Sarvadamana. Then to himself*)

It's my limbs that
thrill, touched

by the little heir
of some stranger

What fulfilment must
he cause in the mind

of the achiever
from whose lap he grew

SECOND WOMAN: (*Observes both*) Wow, interesting.

DUṢYANTA: What's it?

SECOND WOMAN: I'm astonished by how similar the boy's looks are to yours. And although you're a stranger, he acts like he is not averse to you.

DUṢYANTA: (*Fondling Sarvadamana*) If he is not the son of a sage, what is his family?

SECOND WOMAN: The Puru family.

DUṢYANTA: (*To himself*) How come, it turns out to be the same as mine. No wonder this lady thinks he looks like me. There is this last family vow of the Purus:

Those who first want to live in
palaces super-sensual places
to protect the territory

They're disciplined later—
A single chaste wife
Tree-bases, their homes

(*Aloud*) But human beings cannot get to this place of their own accord.

SECOND WOMAN: Exactly as you say. His mother—who was related to an apsarā—gave birth to him here, the āśrama of the father of the gods.

DUṢYANTA: (*Aside*) This is a second reason for hope. (*Aloud*) And what's the name of the sage the lady there is wife to?

SECOND WOMAN: Who'll even think of uttering his name who abandoned his legitimate wife!

DUṢYANTA: (*To himself*) This story only points to me. Should I then ask the name of this child's mother? Or is it impolite to ask about another man's wife?

(*The first woman enters with a clay peacock in her hand*)

FIRST WOMAN: Sarvadamana, look at *Śakuntalāvaṇya*, the beauty of the Śakunta bird.

SARVADAMANA: (*Casts a glance*) Where's my mummy?

BOTH WOMEN: Mother's pet, deceived by the similarity in name.

SECOND WOMAN: Darling, you've been told to see the beauty of the Śakunta bird, the clay peacock.

DUṢYANTA: (*To himself*) Is his mother's name Śakuntalā? But there are similarities in names. Like a mirage, the idea of the name may only bring me disappointment.

SARVADAMANA: Mummy, I like this nice peacock. (*Takes the toy*)

FIRST WOMAN: (*Anxious*) Oh, the amulet, it's not on his wrist.

DUṢYANTA: Easy, easy. Here it is, fell from his tussle with the lion-cub. (*Reaches to pick it up*)

BOTH WOMEN: Nooo don't take it! How come he's got it! (*Astonished, hands on chest, Duṣyanta and Sarvadamana look at each other*)

DUṢYANTA: Why was I forbidden?

FIRST WOMAN: Listen, King. This is a herb called Aparājitā, given by Sage Kaśyapa at the birth rites. When it falls to the ground, no one may pick it up, except for the mother, father and child.

DUṢYANTA: What if they pick it up?

FIRST WOMAN: It turns into a serpent and bites the person.

DUṢYANTA: Has this metamorphosis been personally witnessed by you?

BOTH WOMEN: Many times.

DUṢYANTA: (*Happily, to himself*) Why don't I welcome the fulfilment of my desires! (*Hugs Sarvadamana*)

SECOND WOMAN: Suvratā, come here. Let's tell this news to Śakuntalā, busy with her vows.

(*They leave*)

SARVADAMANA: Let me go. I'll go to my mummy.

DUṢYANTA: My child, you'll go with me to greet your mother.

SARVADAMANA: My daddy's Duṣyanta, not you!

DUṢYANTA: (*With a smile*) Even this protest is persuasive.

(*Śakuntalā enters wearing a single plait, customary of a chaste wife whose husband is far away*)

ŚAKUNTALĀ: I heard that Sarvadamana's herb-amulet kept its natural form even in metamorphosis, even then, I did not place hope in my fate. Or, does it turn out as Sānumatī said.

DUṢYANTA: (*Looks at Śakuntalā*) Yes, this lady here is Śakuntalā.

> Dressed in a pair of gray clothes
> Wearing a single braid
>
> Face emaciated by religious vows
>
> Chaste, she bears a long ordeal
> of separation from unkind me

ŚAKUNTALĀ: (*Looks at the king who is pale with remorse*) Not like my husband. Who is this, now, with his body so close to my son, defiling him? My son's protected by an auspicious amulet.

SARVADAMANA: (*Goes to his mother*) Mummy, this man here is hugging me, calling me 'son'.

DUṢYANTA: My love, despite my cruelty, there's a happy ending because of you. Now that I see I've been recognized by you.

ŚAKUNTALĀ: (*To herself*) Heart, relax, relax. Fate gives up jealousy and empathizes with me. This is my husband, yes.

DUṢYANTA: My love.

> Memory scattered the fog of confusion
>
> Thanks to fate, lovely-face
> You're here facing me
>
> At the end of the eclipse the moon
> unites with *his wife, the star*
> Rohiṇī

ŚAKUNTALĀ: Husband, Jai, be a winner, be… (*With a tearful voice, pauses halfway*)

DUṢYANTA:

Hey Lovely,

At the word 'Jai'
        though it was checked by tears
I won, for I saw

Your pouting lips
Pale without cosmetics

SARVADAMANA: Mummy, who's this?

ŚAKUNTALĀ: Darling, ask your Fate.

DUṢYANTA: (*Falls at Śakuntalā's feet*)

Hey Pretty

Remove the pain of rejection
from your heart

My mind was under
some strong spell then

Such behaviour happens
even in auspicious events

under the influence
of severe ignorance

Doubtful, a blind man shakes off
even a garland put on him

ŚAKUNTALĀ: Get up, husband. Surely some bad thing I did before generated its karmic consequences. So my husband, usually pleasant, acted angrily towards me.

(*Duṣyanta gets up*)

ŚAKUNTALĀ: Then how did my husband remember poor-me?

DUṢYANTA: I'll tell you, plucking out the thorn of sadness.

Beautiful,

Once confused I ignored
the teardrops troubling

your lower lip

Now they cling between
your curved eyelashes

I'll wipe them to
be remorseless

(*Does as he says*)

ŚAKUNTALĀ: (*Sees the engraved ring*) That is the ring!

DUṢYANTA: It was because the ring was found that my memory came back.

ŚAKUNTALĀ: It made trouble. It was unavailable when my husband had to be convinced.

DUṢYANTA: Let the vine get the flower back, as a sign of getting together with springtime.

ŚAKUNTALĀ: I don't trust it. Let my husband be the one to wear it.

(*Mātali enters*)

MĀTALI: Thanks to Fate, the king is doing well, reuniting with his wife, seeing his son's face.

DUṢYANTA: My desire has had sweet success. Was this matter not known to Indra?

MĀTALI: Is anything unknown to the gods? Come, king, Sage Kaśyapa grants you a meeting.

DUṢYANTA: Śakuntalā, give our son a hand. I want to see the sage with you in the lead.

ŚAKUNTALĀ: I'm shy to go to my guru with my husband.

DUṢYANTA: But it must be done, in good times.

(*All walk around*)

(*Sage Kaśyapa enters with wife Aditi, aka Dākṣāyiṇī. Kaśyapa sits*)

KAŚYAPA: (*Looks at the king*)

Dākṣāyiṇī,

This is him
called Duṣyanta—King—

Rode in the vanguard
of your son's war.

His bow's task done
makes Indra's

jagged thunderbolt
a showpiece

ADITI: It must be so, it is what I gather from his looks.

MĀTALI: King, these parents of the gods are looking at you with eyes that show parental love. Go near now.

DUṢYANTA:

This is the pair

[Aditi] born to Dakṣa,
[Kaśyapa] born to Marīci

Just one generation removed
from the creator

Brahma's their grandfather

Sages call them
the source of the radiance *the Sun*
divided into twelve forms *of months*

They gave birth to Indra
The god of three worlds *earth, heaven and in-between*
The chief of the gods who eats offerings at vedic rituals

Even he *Viṣṇu*
who's better than the self-existent *Brahma*
chose them as his parents

MĀTALI: You said it.

DUṢYANTA: (*Goes near*) Indra's servant, Duṣyanta, bows to both of you.

KAŚYAPA: Live long. Look after the earth.

ADITI: My dear, be unbeatable.

ŚAKUNTALĀ: I bow to your feet along with my son.

KAŚYAPA:

Your husband's equal to Indra
Son's like Jayanta
No other blessing's necessary
Be like Poulomi [*Indra's wife*]

ADITI: My dear, may you be treated well by your husband. For sure, the child will live long and be a darling of the family. Sit.

(*Everyone sits around Sage Kaśyapa*)

KAŚYAPA: (*Points at them, one by one*)

Thanks to Fate

Śakuntalā's good.
The child's good.
And you are here.

Faith, Wealth, Fortune.
All three come together.

DUṢYANTA: Divine sage, first achieving what I desired. Then seeing you. Your favour's without precedent.

First the flower shows up
Then the fruit

First the dense clouds rise
Only then the rain

This is the sequence
of cause–effect

But your blessing's result
precedes it

MĀTALI: That's the way the gods bless.

DUṢYANTA: Divine sage, I married this protégée of yours in the Gāndharva style. After some time, she was brought to me by her relatives. My memory was poor, I rejected her. I offended Sage Kaṇva, who is of your lineage. Later, upon seeing the ring, I realized that his daughter was married to me. Seems strange to me.

Just as one insists
when it's right there

within view—
'Not an elephant.'

When it has gone—
Doubt.

On seeing its footprints—
Belief.

My mind's shifts were like that.

KAŚYAPA: Stop thinking that you're to blame. You don't even get the blame of 'delusion' or 'confusion'. Listen.

DUṢYANTA: I'm all ears.

KAŚYAPA: Even when Menakā went down to Apsaratīrtha and brought Śakuntalā—who was evidently in trouble—to Dākṣāyiṇī's side, I understood what had really happened using my yogic powers. This chaste woman and legitimate wife was rejected by you because of Durvāsa's curse, and for no other reason. And that ended with the vision of the ring.

DUṢYANTA: (*With a sigh*) I'm free from blame.

ŚAKUNTALĀ: (*To herself*) Thank heavens. I wasn't rejected by my husband for no reason. But I don't remember being cursed. Or, the curse that was put on me didn't register as I was absent-minded by my separation from the king. So that's why my friends told me, 'Show the ring to your husband.'

KAŚYAPA: You know the history now. Don't think it was all your husband's doing. See:

Because of the curse
you were spurned

Because of a memory loss
your husband, cruel

Now that the fog has gone
You're on top again

A reflection does not form
when dirt blocks clarity

But on a clean mirror
It forms easily

DUṢYANTA: As you say, divine sage.

KAŚYAPA: Did you greet your son by Śakuntalā? We did his birth rites.

DUṢYANTA: Divine sage, my lineage depends on him. (*Holds the boy by his hand*)

KAŚYAPA: It will be so. King, know that he's an Emperor. See:

Crossing the sea by chariot
with an even and steady pace

Unbeatable, he conquers
the seven continents on earth

Now he's 'Sarvadamana'
For he controls all creatures firmly

Later he gets the name 'Bharata'
by sustaining the world

DUṢYANTA: We have high hopes in him, whose rituals were done by your divine self.

ADITI: Divine sage, now that daughter's wishes have been fulfilled, do send word to Kaṇva. And Menakā, who's so fond of her daughter, roams right here.

ŚAKUNTALĀ: The divine lady has expressed my desire.

KAŚYAPA: Everything's evident to him by his yogic power.

DUṢYANTA: No wonder the sage was not so angry with me.

KAŚYAPA: Anyway, he'll get the good news from me. (*Speaks to someone outside*) Is anyone around?

GĀLAVA (*enters*): I'm here, divine sage.

KAŚYAPA: Gālava, go by air right away and, on my behalf, tell Sage Kaṇva the good news. That daughter Śakuntalā has been accepted by Duṣyanta whose memory returned at the end of the curse.

GĀLAVA: As the divine sage says. (*Leaves*)

KAŚYAPA: You, too, get on your friend Indra's chariot, and go to your capital with your wife and son.

DUṢYANTA: As the divine sage says. (*Doesn't leave*)

KAŚYAPA: What else can I do for you, what would you like?

DUṢYANTA: Is there anything better than this! If the divine sage here wants to do a favour, let it be this:

May the king strive
for the good of the people
and nature

May the speech of vedic-savants
Sarasvatī
be valued

May the bluish-reddish
self-existent *Śiva*
whose power's everywhere

End my rebirth

(*Everyone leaves*)

END OF ACT VII

from

ṚTUSAṂHĀRAM

A Collection of Seasons

As those who live in the Indian regions know, there are not four seasons, but six—no autumn or fall after spring and summer, but a rainy season, a brief period of sultry after the rains, and of frost before winter sets in. Kālidāsa's poem, *Ṛtusaṃhāram*, describes how these changing seasons impact an entire spectrum of life, from trees to elephants, snakes, birds, bees and humans. The poem has some classic images we have now come to see as clichéd—clouds longing for mountains and breezes nuzzling flowers; but, we also encounter refreshing similes, perhaps, which dropped out of use—rivers like brazen women, for instance. The mood of *Ṛtusaṃhāram* is exuberant and playful, nature is not dangerous, frogs inadvertently hop under a snake's hood, or get nervous about snaking rivulets, but nothing cheerless occurs. Nature is distinctly feminine for the poet, and the analogies weave back and forth between the physical beauty of women and the beauty of the natural environment; and when nature competes with women, it can also surpass them. In many of the stanzas, the poet directly addresses a lover.

Ṛtusaṃhāram tends to be the least admired of works attributed to Kālidāsa. While some scholars have concluded that it cannot possibly be Kālidāsa's, some others suggest it must be juvenilia. Kālidāsa's poetry usually calls for painstaking attention. You begin with a grammatical analysis and rearrange the parts of a stanza in a coherent order. Once you have 'got' it, only then do you soak it in. The intricate and multiple relationships between the parts of the stanza allow for repeated reading and appreciation. It's amazing how everything is exact and coordinated, a sophisticated machine, wheels within wheels.

Ṛtusaṃhāram has none of that. While there are clusters of relationships, these clusters don't quite interact with each other. The syntax is straightforward, easy for a beginner to follow. See Stanza 19 from the 'Rain' section of the poem—one line of verbs in the plural and one line of nouns in the plural. Literally: They flow - they rain - they roar - they shine - they remember - they dance - they take shelter. The next line names the nouns that perform these actions. This is like an elementary school exercise. And yet, translated into English, laid out in columns, it has a vaguely charming simplicity—how tempting to jumble them up and pose a mix 'n' match question! Stanza 2 in 'Sultry Season' is also straightforward, a string of relationships defined by the instrumental case ending. What brings unity to this stanza is that every particular is whitish—grass, moonbeams, swans—it's as if these objects have taken over the landscape—earth, night, lake—with their whiteness, possessed it. What actually happens because of this relationship? The earth does nothing with the grass, it's just made lovelier by it. In the English translation, I use the connector 'by' instead of 'with', thus extending the instrumentality towards a sense of attribution, or authorship: not just 'earth with Kāśa blossoms', but 'earth by Kāśa blossoms'.

This next chapter has some delightful verses from each of the seasons of *Ṛtusaṃhāram*. In the translation, the stanzas of *Ṛtusaṃhāram* shift into the genre of fragments. Each fragment presents a single delightful thing—a woman dressing up, or a cute soundplay in 'Kiṃśuka' and the 'Aṃśuka'. If the Sanskrit stanzas of *Ṛtusaṃhāram* do not deliver profound aesthetic delight, they become delectable in the English translation as minimalistic, carefully laid-out impressionistic vignettes.

SUMMER

1.

My Love,

Summer's here burning

Sun a scorching scourge
Moon desirable

Rainwater pools for anytime-dips

Dusk agreeable

Kāma mellow

18.

A frog jumps tortured by sharp sunrays
out of a dirty pond

sits under the parasol-
hood

of a thirsty cobra

22.

A keen forest fire crop-shoots withered

Fast furious winds dry leaves flung up

In the sun's heat all around shrunken waters

Watching at forest edges
High Anxiety

23.

Birds pant
on dry-leaved trees

Tired monkeys take
to mountain shrubs

Bulls roam everywhere
Want water

Elephants extend trunks
into water wells

RAIN

1.

My dear,

Cloud Misty's here
The love of lovers

A rather high and mighty entry
like a king

Thunder drums
Lightning flag

Ruttish elephant

7.

Like immodest women unrestrained

Rivers speedy agitated currents
felling trees on banks as they
rush
to the sea

8.

Fresh rainwater
full of termites dirt grass
sallow

snakes downwards

A snake-y crooked gait

Frogs watch
worried

19.

flow Rivers

rain Clouds

roar Ruttish elephants

shine Forest edges

remember Parted lovers

dance	Peacocks
seekshelter	Monkeys

SULTRY SEASON

2.

Bleached

Earth	by	Kāśa blossoms
Nights		the moon
River waters		swans
Lakes		lilies
Forest edges		flower laden Saptacchadā trees
Gardens		Mālatī blossoms

7.

Night matures
like a wild young girl
day by day

She wears
choice jewellery star-clusters
silken moonlight

Moon-face freed from cloud-veil

22.

Surpassed!

Women's graceful gait
by swans

Radiant moon-faces
by full-blown lotuses

Eyes
by blue lotuses

Eyebrow-coquetry
by nicely rippling waves

FROST

1.

Here
Grain-sprouts shot up delightful
Full-flowered Lodhra tree
Paddy ripe and ready
Dew dropped
Wilted lotuses
The frost season's arrived

5.

Women prep for sex fests

Smear turmeric on limbs
Etch leaf designs on lotus-like faces
Perfume hair in black-aloe smoke

14.

Some young woman
prettifies her lotus-like face

in the mirror
in the morning sun

scrutinizes lips her lover sucked
his teeth-tip bites

15.

Another

body weary from too much sex
lotus-eyes red from waking all night

hair awry loose around her shoulders

tries to sleep
warmed by a mild sunray

WINTER

1.

Hey choice-thighs,

The earth covered reverberates

heaps of paddy a Krauñca-bird warble
and sugarcane someplace

Lots of passion
Women love it!

hear,
winter's here

2.

Now's when

People shut windows
stay in

go to
fire sunrays sweaters nubile women

3.

Not moonlight cool sandal-paste

terraces cool as autumn-moon

winds chill with fresh snowflakes

Now
none of these
appeal to people's minds

4.

The nights

cool from thick dew-fall cooled by moon-rays

decked in bright star-clusters

No use to people

SPRING

21.

All over

Kiṃśuka forests' hanging blossoms like
wind-shaken fire-flames

The earth glows

Like a new spring-sprung bride in red robes aṃśuka

22.

Why
does this cuckoo try
with melodious warble

to steal the minds of youth?

Are they not already

loaded   by pretty faces
poked   by Kiṃśuka (*why-parrot*) flowers   the colour of parrots' beaks
seared   by Karṇikāra (*ear-piercing*) blossoms

23.

Happy vague warble of male cuckoos
Murmur of tipsy buzzing bees

Disturb
even   the hearts of
brides   bashful and timid

though in their husband's home

from

RAGHUVAṂŚAM

The Raghu Dynasty

In nineteen cantos, *Raghuvaṃśam* recounts the lives of twenty-eight kings of the solar dynasty of Raghu, including that of King Rāma, the celebrated and worshipped hero of the Indian epic Rāmāyaṇa. The poem may be categorized under the Sanskrit literary genre of 'mahākāvya', which literally means a great or major poem. A mahākāvya takes its themes from such epic histories as the Rāmāyaṇa or Mahābhārata. The seventh-century CE poet, Bhāmaha, defines a mahākāvya by these features: considerable length, a grand plot built around a great personality, and language that is embellished and profound rather than commonplace.

The story of *Raghuvaṃśam* begins with King Dilīpa and Queen Sudakṣiṇā, childless due to a curse. On propitiating a sacred cow, they are blessed with a son, Raghu. Raghu is born in Canto II and goes on to perform a hundred horse sacrifices, threatening the position of Indra, chief of the gods. This results in a battle, resolved by a compromise; Raghu receives the full merits of the sacrifice and Indra keeps his position. Canto IV is about Raghu's greatness and noble qualities, and has descriptions of battles, military campaigns and the borders of Raghu's kingdom. A well-known anecdote from Canto V is about a brahmin student who needs money to pay a substantial fee of gratitude to his teacher. Due to excessive charity, Raghu does not have the resources, and decides to raid Kubera, treasurer of the gods; the mere threat prompts Kubera to quickly make the money available. The brahmin's blessing secures Raghu a son named Aja. Aja is also a prince to reckon with, and has his own adventures, one of which results in the reward of a magic weapon. Canto VI describes the svayamvara of the princess of Vidarbha, Indumati, wherein she selects her groom from among a gathering of illustrious kings. When Indumati favours Aja, the other competing kings conspire against him, and the magic weapon saves the day. Canto VII describes their wedding. Canto VIII brings us to Aja's son, Daśaratha, who later becomes the father of Rāma. Canto IX narrates a hunting accident which results in a curse—that Daśaratha will die from the shock of separation from his son, thus setting up the story of the Rāmāyaṇa.

Cantos X to XV narrate the story of Rāma. Interestingly, many events that are described in great detail in the Vālmīki Rāmāyaṇa are rather sketchy in *Raghuvaṃśam.* In Canto XII, Kālidāsa summarizes five entire chapters from Vālmīki's version in a few stanzas. One wonders if such an abridgement is because the legendary story of Rāma would already be well known to audiences. Canto XII lingers in great detail over Rāma's return journey from Laṅka. Thus, unlike the title of Rāmāyaṇa, which suggests a focus on the 'going' (ayana) of Rāma, Kālidāsa dwells on Rama's return.

Canto XVI covers the life of Kuśa, who re-establishes Ayodhyā as the capital. Canto XVII praises Atithi, and Canto XVIII covers twenty-one kings. Canto XIX describes a licentious King Agnivarṇa, and ends, somewhat abruptly. Also, other genealogies in the Indian tradition enumerate dozens more kings in the Raghu dynasty after Agnivarṇa; therefore, *Raghuvaṃśam* is regarded incomplete. The next chapter is a translation of Canto I, which begins with Kālidāsa's renowned invocation to Śiva and Pārvatī and is followed by a fascinating description of a Raghu king's dharma.

CANTO I

JOURNEY TO VASIṢṬHA'S HERMITAGE

1.

To make words meaningful I
Invoke Śiva–Pārvatī—

Makers of the world
Like word and meaning wed

2.

My theme the Solar Dynasty
My talent not more than dim

Folly! wanting to cross
an ocean on a raft

3.

Seeking fame reserved for poets
I'm a dunce I'm going to be mocked

like a dwarf
Arms greed-stretched for fruit
only the tall can reach

4.

Or perhaps I'll enter through the door of speech
opened by previous poets

Easy

Like a thread through a gem
already pierced by a diamond

5–9.

That's me.

Although deficient in speech

When their virtues come to my ears
I'm compelled

I will dare describe
The Raghu dynasty:

All the way from birth, pure
All the way to celestial regions their chariots
All the way to the edges of oceans their kingdoms
All the way until results are evident their duties

Their rituals follow rules
Punishments suit crimes
Gifts meet desires
Their attention's on time

For charity's sake, wealth
For truth's sake, brevity
For fame's sake, victory
Only for propagation, marriage

In boyhood they study
In youth they relish the world
In old age they are ascetics

And at the end they
forsake their bodies, yogic

10.

People who know the difference
between wrong and right,

Listen to this story.

It's in fire that gold's tested.
Pure, or alloyed?

11.

Once upon a time
A king called Manu

Vaivasvata's son
Respected by men

First among kings
Like 'Om' among chants

12.

In that pure family
A purer one born

His name, Dilīpa
A shining king

Like a moon born
in a milky ocean

13.

Broad-chested
Stout shoulders bullish

Giant arms
Tall as a palmyra tree

Kṣatriya dharma personified
A body ready for its job

14.

He stood over the earth like Mt. Meru

His radiance
His quintessence
Surpassed everyone else's

15.

As smart as he was handsome
As learned as he was smart
As driven as he was learned
As successful as he was driven

16.

Awesome kingly traits for his people

Inviting as well as formidable
Like the ocean
with gems and monsters both

17.

His people
Tyre-tracks

They did not swerve from his steering
Never off the beaten path begun by *ancestor* Manu
Not even by a hairline

18.

He collected taxes from his people
in their own interest

Sun takes water
Rains a thousand times over

19.

Army, just an extra frill

To get things done
he had two:

Mind steeped in sciences
String stretched on a bow

20.

Ministerial meetings hush-hush
Gestures cryptic

From outcomes infer his ventures

Like past lives from this life's
predispositions

21.

Fearless and yet protected himself
Not sickly and yet did good deeds
Not greedy and yet collected taxes
Detached and yet lived it up

22.

Wise yet silent
Powerful yet patient
Charitable but refraining from self-praise

Coming together in him
Contrary traits seemed siblings

23.

He was not drawn to objects of desire
Mastered the far reaches of knowledge
Delighted in doing the right thing

Therefore grew old without ageing

24.

Controlling
Protecting
Sustaining
He was father to his people

Their real fathers were simply birth-tools

25.

He punished the guilty for order's sake
Married only for procreation's sake

So for this best of men
Even the pursuit of wealth and pleasure
was actually dharma

26.

He milked the cow of the earth
for vedic sacrifices

Indra tapped the skies for rain
for the growth of crops

This mutual exchange sustained
both the worlds

27.

Other Kings could not keep up
with his reputation for protection

'Theft' left what belonged to others
Stayed as a word in the vocabulary

28.

A good man was welcome even if venomous
As medicine to one who's sick

If wicked, even a friend was to be severed
Like a cobra-bitten finger

29.

Uniting primary elements
Ether Air Fire Water Earth
The Creator designed him

So all his traits were used
for only one result:

The welfare of others

30.

He ruled the earth as if
it were a single city

Shores, its ramparts
Ocean, its moat

It had no other ruler

31.

He had a wife named Sudakṣiṇā

Daughter of the Magadha dynasty
Her name accrued from her traits

Like 'dakṣiṇā' the consort and gift
of a vedic sacrifice

32.

Though the ruler of the earth had a large harem
He thought of himself as a married man

Married to this virtuous woman
And the goddess of fortune

33.

Keen that she, his alter-ego,
bear a son

He passed his time hopefully
Though fulfilment was delayed

34.

To do rituals for a son
He took the heavy yoke of the world
Off from his shoulders
And entrusted it to his ministers

35.

Then, bathed, invoking the Creator for a son,
The couple went to Vasiṣṭha guru's hermitage

36.

They rode a chariot
A soft, deep rattle

Like Indra's elephant Airāvata and Lightning
on a rain-bearing cloud

37.

Thinking 'let there be no disturbance to the hermitage'
They took a limited retinue

But from their distinct aura
It was as if an army surrounded them

38.

Fanned by tingling breezes fragrant with
Śāla-trees' exhalations
Pollen scattered from shaken forest-groves

39.

They heard coos like the split
double note ṣaḍja *of Indian music*

Delightful

Peacocks raising necks
at the sound of chariot rims

40.

They saw the similarity of their own mutual glances
in the eyes of pairs of deer

The deer shifted away but not too far
Eyes riveted on the smooth-moving chariot

41.

They raised faces sometimes
at melodious crane calls

Cranes in formation
Like a door-garland unsupported by a post

42.

The breeze, favourable
A sign that their wishes would be fulfilled

The dust flung up by the horses' hooves
didn't touch their headgear

43.

They inhaled

The scent of lake-lotuses
Cool from ripples

They inhaled it like
their own breath

44.

In villages marked by signposts of vedic sacrifices
Villages they'd themselves founded

They received a welcome
Followed by the sure blessings of ritualists

45.

Of old country folk who brought fresh butter
and lingered

They asked the names of wild roadside trees

46.

What grandeur

Set out in bright clothes they were like
the moon and the star Citrā
after the frost

47.

The ruler of the earth showed his wife
his favourite sights

He was Buddha-like *knew everything*
but did not know

How far they had come

48.

Hard-earned fame
He arrived

at the hermitage of the disciplined sage
in the evening

with his wife and tired horses

49.

The hermitage filled up

with ascetics returning from the forest-depths
with Kuśa grass, fruit, food and kindling

Invisible sacred fires rose

50.

Like children, lots of deer

blocked the doors of huts for their share
of Nīvāra grains strewn by ascetics' wives

51.

Ascetics' daughters watered plants
Stepped away at once so
Birds could drink from tree basins
without apprehension

52.

At daylight's end

Heaps of wild rice
Deer squatted on the ground in the yards of huts
chewing cud

53.

Smoke—*sign of fire*—flung up by the breeze
Wind-shaken scent of oblations' incense

purified guests about to enter

54.

The king directed the charioteer
'Give the horses some rest'

He got off and helped his wife alight

55.

The group of ascetics with disciplined senses
welcomed him and his consort

Wise protector
He deserved the honour

56.

At the end of the evening rituals he saw

Penance-rich Vasiṣṭha with Aruṇdhati
sitting behind him

Like vedic fire-god Agni
and wife Svāhā

57.

The king and the queen, the daughter
of the Magadha dynasty,

touched the feet of Vasiṣṭha and his wife
who blessed them lovingly

58.

Soothing the fatigue of the chariot ride
with hospitality

The sage asked the sagely king
about the well-being of his kingdom

59.

In front of Sage Vasiṣṭha
Rich in the *Atharvaveda*

The king began to speak
meaningfully

The king
The best of men
The conqueror of the cities of enemies
Meaningful words, his wealth

60.

'Good, of course, in all my seven parts
of state: king, ministry, allies, treasury
kingdom, fortresses, army

You squash the troubles
God or man-made

61.

'Chanter of mantras,

When my enemies are subdued
by your mantras from far

As if my arrows are recalled

My arrows that split a target
near enough to be
seen

62.

'Vedic ritualist,

The oblation you offer the vedic fire
with the right procedures

becomes rain for crops
that would otherwise be dry

63.

'If my people live long lives
without fear and disease

It's thanks to your austere power

64.

'How could my wealth not be trouble-free

When I've constantly been looked after
by my guru, a descendant of the creator?

65.

'But to me who has not seen
your daughter-in-law's worthy child

This earth with gem-bearing islands
does not appeal

66.

'Foreseeing a break in offerings after my death

The spirits of my ancestors don't eat
as freely as they'd like
Saving it for later

67.

'My ancestral spirits warm with their sighs
The libations of water I offer

Thinking it hard to get when I'm gone

68.

'Brightened by vedic rituals
Darkened by the lack of a child

That's who I am
Shining and not-shining

Like the mountain Lokāloka
One side bright, other side dark

69.

'Happiness in the other world is born
from good deeds, penance and charity

Comfort in this as well as the next
requires a child of pure ancestry

70.

'This lack of a child
How come you see and don't feel bad

A plant of the hermitage you watered yourself
Fruitless?

71.

'The suffering's unbearable, Sir
This last debt of mine
debt to ancestors, repaid by having a son

Like a tie-post that pierces the guts
of an elephant deprived of a bath

72.

'Father, do what you've got to do to free me

When something's hard to get for Ikṣvāku kings
Success depends on you.'

73.

Told so by the king

The sage remained meditative for a moment
Eyes still

Like a tank of sleeping fish

74.

He saw with his yogic powers the reason
for the suppression of offspring

Clairvoyant from yogic practice the sage
Told the ruler of the earth about it

thus:

75.

'Long ago when you returned from waiting on Indra

En route was the divine cow 'Surabhi'
under the wish-fulfilling tree

76.

'Musing over the queen who'd just finished her period
Anxious to do your *sexual*
dharma

You didn't do well by Surabhi
Worthy of circumambulation

77.

'She cursed you—

"You ignore me
So you will not have a child
without first worshipping my child."

78.

'Neither you nor your charioteer heard the curse
It was noisy

Divine elephants who guard directions played
in the current of the celestial river Gaṅgā,
the milky way

79.

'Be aware, your desire's prevented
from that neglect

A lapse in worshipping the worthy
limits your glory

80.

'She's now in the underworld for butter oblations
for the long vedic ritual of Pracetas

Gates guarded by serpents

81.

'Regard her daughter as her representative

Purify yourself
Worship her with your wife

When pleased, she grants desires
like milk.'

82.

As he spoke this, the faultless cow named Nandinī
returned from the forest

Nandinī's instrumental in vedic rituals
for ritualist Vasiṣṭha

83.

She has the rosy sheen of a young leaf
Wears a white curved tuft on her forehead

Like twilight wears a fresh moon

84.

Pitcher-udder
Flows at the sight of her calf
Rains warm milk on earth

More potent than the last bath of vedic rituals

85.

The dust flung up by her hooves touched
the limbs of the king nearby

The purification she gave the king
Like bathing in holy places

86.

A holy sight
Seeing her

The penance-rich sage who could read signs
told the king again

His stated desire would not be unfulfilled

87.

'Figure it out, King
Your success is not far

The moment her name's praised
This blessed cow's here

88.

'You must live in the forest
Serve this cow constantly

Gratify her
Like one gratifies Knowledge
with studious exercises

89.

'Walk when she walks
Stand when she stands
Sit when she sits

When she drinks water, you drink water

90.

'After worshipping Surabhi in the morning

May our pure, devoted daughter-in-law
follow her as far as the penance-grove

And go back in the evening to receive her

91.

'Follow her thus
until she's happy

May you be trouble-free
Stand like a father
First among those with sons.'

92.

'As you say.'

Knowing the right time and place
for *the guru's* guidance

The disciple bowed
Accepted happily with his wife

93.

In the evening, the creator's son Vasiṣṭha
Prudent
Speaker of truth

Dismissed the king whose fortune had awoken
to go to bed

94.

Although the sage had yogic powers
He considered the *king's* vow

Using his creative power he materialized
Only rustic accommodation

95.

The king and his partner, his pious wife

Stayed in a hut of leaves
shown by the family guru

Spent the night on a bed
of Kuśa grass

Two disciples chanting vedas
announced its conclusion

END OF CANTO I

from

KUMĀRASAMBHAVAM

The Birth of Kumāra

Śiva's asceticism after the death of his wife Satī is well-known, so when Tārakāsura, a pesky titan in Hindu mythology, earned a boon from Brahma, he asked that he could only be killed by Śiva's son. Naturally, this necessitates Śiva to break his penance and get interested in love once more. The gods despatch the god of love, Kāma, to influence Śiva.

In seventeen cantos, the story of this poem, *Kumārasambhavam*, covers the romance of Śiva and Pārvatī, the birth of their son Kumāra, and the death of Tāraka. Many scholars have expressed doubts about the authorship of the remaining cantos, in particular because eminent fourteenth century CE commentator Mallinātha only covered eight cantos. The first eight cantos cover events leading up to the birth of Kumāra. Canto I opens in the setting of the Himālayas; Pārvatī is the daughter of Himavān, the mountain king. When Sage Nārada meets Pārvatī, he recognizes at once that she is Satī reborn and lets her parents know just who will be her husband. Himavān sends Pārvatī to serve Śiva while he is engaged in deep meditation, and in the process, Pārvatī finds herself falling in love. Into this scene arrives Kāma, who is successful in his mission. Śiva is disturbed, attracted to Pārvatī, but also furious with Kāma; he opens his third eye and burns Kāma to ashes. An embarrassed Pārvatī leaves and takes up penance herself; Śiva finds her and successfully woos her. They marry.

The poem's locations are mystical and unearthly—the Himālayas; the world of Brahma; the court of Indra; Kailāsa where Śiva resides, and so on. Into these settings, Kālidāsa brings entirely human emotions and detail—springtime in the mountains, Pārvatī's beauty, the lament of Kāma's wife Rati in Canto IV, the humorous frisson in the conversation between Śiva and Pārvatī in Canto V, the spectacle as well as domestic detail of their elaborate wedding in Canto VII, and then the descriptions of their love-making—which has gathered much discussion of whether such carnal detail is tasteful, or just audacious. The canto translated here features the legendary and pivotal moment from the drama of the temptation of Śiva by Kāma.

CANTO III

THE BURNING OF KĀMA

1.

Suddenly the thousand eyes of Indra
turned from the thirty gods

And fell on Kāma

The attention chiefs pay subordinates
usually depends on their uses

2.

'Sit here.'

So Kāma sat
near Indra's high seat

Nodded acknowledgement
of his superior's favour

Began to speak
in private

3.

'Your favour—your
attention—I want

to make more of it
with your orders

You're smart
Ask for whatever

in the worlds it is that
must be done for you

4.

'If your annoyance comes
from one who performs

a long, grave penance
seeking your position

Right-on, he's the target
of my bow, arrow ready

5.

'If someone dares step

on the path of liberation
without your permission

for fear of suffering
recurring birth

May he remain chained
for a long time

by sidelong glances shot
by the arched eyebrows

of lovely women

6.

'Say! Who shall I torture
among your enemies?

Even if trained by the wise
demon-chief Uśanas

in the rules of success
and righteousness

I'll destroy

like the Sindhu river
destroys banks

I'll use passion
My secret agent

7.

'Who's the chaste beauty
with a shapely behind

who took over your roving heart
who you wish would fling

her arms around your neck
of her own free will

shamelessly?

8.

'Who, irate, spurned
you, lustful,

fallen at her feet?
I'll make her suffer

So bad her body will ache
for a bed of tender leaves

9.

'Relax, great hero, give
your thunderbolt a break

Whoever the god-foe

His strong arms weak
by my weapons

He will fear even the peeved
lower-lip-pouts of women

10.

'Thanks to your blessings, though

my weapons are but flowers
and my aide's just Spring

I'll snub the gall of
trident-armed Śiva

Who are the bowmen
better than me?'

11.

Indra moved his leg off his thigh
Graced a stool with his foot

Said to Kāma

who'd so openly declared
his talent for the task

12.

'All of that is possible
for you my friend

I have two weapons:
The thunderbolt and you

The thunderbolt is useless
on those with yogic powers

But you do get around
successfully

13.

'I know your resources
So I entrust you

with a task as important
for me to accomplish

Figuring that *legendary serpent* Śeṣa
Could lift the earth

Kṛṣṇa directed Śeṣa
to carry him

14.

'Boasting how
your bow can track

bull-rider Śiva
you have a headstart

on our plan. This
is exactly what

the gods have in mind
as they face strong foes

I mean the gods who share
in the offerings of vedic rituals
Śiva gets no share

15.

'These gods hope
for a hero

born from Śiva's essence
to conquer armies

A single shot from you upon
Śiva, born of Brahma,

third-eye absorbed in Brahman,
And that's possible

16.

'Try to get self-controlled Śiva to like
Pārvatī, devout daughter of Himālaya

According to self-born Brahma
Only she among women has

a strong womb for Śiva
to impregnate

17.

'And as directed by her father

The Mountain's daughter serves
immovable Śiva

Up there
Meditating

I heard it from the very mouths
of the apsarās, they're my spies

18.

'So go. Accomplish
the gods' mission.

Its goal depends
on another that waits

on you, the first
provocateur

Like a seed waits
on water to sprout

19.

'You're the lucky one

whose arrows gain
the victory of the gods

An extraordinary act
to produce a fame

as yet unknown

20.

'These supplicants—
none other than the gods

The task—
good for the three worlds

Your job's to be done by the bow—
not too violent at all

What a hero—
Enviable.

21.

'Heart-stirrer Kāma,

Unasked the Spring season
goes along with you

No one can ask the breeze:
go, play with fire.'

22.

'Fine.'

Kāma took his master's orders
on his head like a garland

Began to leave. Indra patted
his body with hands rough

from stroking Airāvata
his pet elephant

23.

To get the job done even
at the risk of his body

Kāma went to Śiva's place
in the Himālayas

With friend Spring, with consort
Rati who followed hesitantly

24.

Spring, the pride of
mind-born desire, Kāma,

Took shape in that forest

For self-controlled
ascetics in meditation

Inconvenient

25.

Unduly the hot-rayed sun
began to move north

The southern direction released
fragrant breezes, like improper sighs

Sun, a vagrant lover
South, a pining girlfriend

26.

Abruptly the Aśoka tree
burst into blossoms and sprigs

all along its branches
even without waiting for

the contact of pretty women's feet
in tinkling anklets

27.

As soon as Kāma finished

Spring placed Kāma's name
on an arrow of mango-blossoms

and nice new leaves
with bees

28.

Though the Karṇikāra flower
flaunts its colours

The heart aches
at its odourlessness

In general, that's the way
of the creator. Averse

to making anything
fully endowed

29.

When the forest mated
with its lover Spring

Scarlet Palāśa blossoms
showed up suddenly

Like a crescent moon, unbloomed,
Like nail marks on foliage

30.

The spirit of Spring showed
Her face

dotted with bees-eyeliner
and a pretty mark

Lips decorated in the soft pink hues
of new mango-shoots

31.

Blinded by Priyāla tree flower pollen
The deer leapt intoxicated upwind

In forests where dry leaves rustled

32.

The male cuckoo
that cooed melodiously

from the sweet sap
of mango sprouts

Its song seemed
the voice of Kāma

able to cut through
the conceit of women

33.

Yakṣa women
at the end of frost

Vivid lips and pale
complexions

Now exude sweat
over their make-up

34.

Noting the untimely arrival
of Spring, ascetics who lived

in the forests of Śiva
struggled to control

the pent-up agitations
of their hearts

somehow

35.

When Kāma got there
together with Rati

Bow fitted with
floral arrows

Pairs showed excessive affection
full of emotion, actively:

36.

A bee sucked honey
from the same flower-cup

as his mate, miming her.
An antelope rubbed his female

with antlers as she, ecstatic,
closed her eyes

37.

An elephant handed a
mouthful of water

fragrant with lotus pollen
to her male

A Cakravāka bird gifted
a half-eaten lotus stalk

to his female with much
feeling

38.

In between songs a celestial
kissed his lover's

tired, sweat-lined face
Make-up a little awry

Eyes lolling from
flower-wine

39.

Trees embraced by vines—brides
pliant branches—arms

Flower bunch—bosom
Trembling lip—leaf buds

40.

Right then

Although hearing
the songs of apsarās

Śiva stayed transcendent
in meditation

Disturbances do not interrupt
the focus

of those who are masters
of themselves

41.

At the entrance of the creeper-bower
A golden cane in his left hand

A finger on his mouth
Nandī made a sign

to Śiva's troops:
'Don't be naughty.'

42.

At that command

The entire forest
froze like a painting

Unshaking trees
Soundless bees

Silent birds, animals
quiet, unmoving

43.

Avoiding his sight

As the sight of Venus
when travelling

Kāma entered Śiva's
meditation space

Lined with thick branches
of Nameru trees

44.

Body soon-to-be
annihilated

Kāma saw
three-eyed Śiva

Self-controlled
Clad in tiger skin

Seated on the platform
of a Devadāru tree

45.

Cross-legged
Steady

Stretched torso

Bent shoulders

Palms opened like
a full-blown lotus

46.

Dreadlocks tied up
by a serpent

Two-string rudrākṣa chain
at his earlobes

Tangled deerskin, bluer
from the hue of his neck

47.

Fierce, steady eyes
Indifferent to

Quivering brows
Flickering eyelashes

Barely open, vision
pointed at nose tip

48.

Controlling breaths

Like a full-cloud
Rainless

Like a lake
Unrippling

Like a lamp, steady
without breeze

49.

Inner channels found
by the third eye

Light rises
from his crown

Pales a young moon's
glow

more tender than
lotus fibres

50.

A mind mastered by yoga
Anchored in the centre

Nine gates of senses restrained
He found in himself what

those in the know know
as 'eternal'

51.

From not too far
Kāma saw

Odd-eyed Śiva
Unassailable

Didn't notice how bow
and arrow slipped

from his fear-shaken
hands

52.

Then the daughter of
the Mountain King

came along with two
woodland deities

Kāma's bravado
Almost blown out

was revived
by her beauty

53.

Springtime flowers
The jewellery she wore

Aśoka more red
than rubies

Alluring Karṇikāra
brighter than gold

Sindhuvāra to mock
a string of pearls

54.

Stooped a little as if
from an ample bosom

Wore clothes the colour of
the morning sun

Like a young, meandering
vine, curvy with

abundant flower clusters

55.

A girdle of Kesara flowers
at her hips

As if Kāma's second bowstring
in the rightful place

Again and again she
pulled it up as it slipped

56.

As bees hovered at
her lower lip, their

desire spiked by
fragrant breath

She drove them off
with her playful lotus,

alarmed, eyes darting
continually

57.

On seeing her
Every limb

Faultless, beauty
surpassing Rati's

Flower-arrowed Kāma
felt hopeful again

of the success of his mission
over the conqueror of senses

and trident-wielder
Śiva

58.

And Pārvatī arrived at the
threshold of her future

husband Śiva.
Meanwhile, seeing

The highest self
The ultimate light

He emerged
from meditation

59.

Slowly he released
his yogic breathing

Relaxed his cross-legged
tight posture

Even as serpent Śeṣa
somehow carried

on his hoods
the weight of the earth

60.

Nandī bowed to Śiva
Announced

Pārvatī's arrival
to wait on him

A mere eyebrow sign
from his master granted

permission to enter
Nandī let her in

61.

First her two friends
bowed

Then at Śiva's feet
they scattered
A handpicked heap of
flowers, new leaf bits

Marking winter's end

62.

Pārvatī too bowed to
bull-rider Śiva

So low the new leaf-shoot
fell from her ear

The fresh Karṇikāra flowers
in her blue-black hair slipped

63.

'Get a husband who
will not love another.'

Śiva blessed her
He just noted a fact

What the gods say
never has results

to the contrary
in this world

64.

And Kāma waits

for the opportune
arrow-moment

Like a fly eager
to enter fire

Again and again he
touches his bowstring

Pārvatī's near Śiva
The target's set

65.

Then, with delicate hands,
Pārvatī offered the

King of Hills
Śiva the ascetic

A rosary of sun-dried beads
from Gangetic lotuses

66.

Soft on devotees
Three-eyed Śiva

Reached out to accept it
Right then

Flower-shooter Kāma
fixed to his bow

The unerring arrow
called 'infatuation'

67.

Śiva too

Gravity faded like
ocean waves at moonrise

Śiva's eyes roved over
Pārvatī's Bimba-fruit-red lips

68.

Pārvatī too

Limbs in goosebumps
like a budding Kadamba tree

Averted face, lovelier
Eyes darting

Pārvatī stood overcome
with feeling

69.

Then with difficulty
Odd-eyed Śiva

Using yogic power
Regained mastery

of agitated senses
Scanned all directions

for the cause of his
mind's transformations

70.

Out of the corner
of his right eye

Śiva saw
self-born Kāma

Fist clenched
Shoulders bent

Left foot drawn back
Bow nicely arched

Ready
to shoot

71.

Meditation assaulted
Rage rose

Twisted eyebrows
A terrifying face to see

All at once from
his third eye

Fire shot out
Blazing

72.

'Calm down,
restrain the anger.'

Voices of *storm-gods* Maruts
in the skies

By then the fire born
of Śiva's eye

had reduced Kāma
to ash

73.

The disaster's impact
Intense

Senses numbed
Rati swooned

It seemed as if a favour
to be momentarily unaware

of her husband's death

74.

Destroying the obstacle
to meditation, Kāma

As a thunderbolt destroys
a tree, swiftly

Chief of beings, Śiva, left
with his followers

to avoid the proximity
of women

75.

Her father's dreams
dashed

Her own grace and
beauty futile

All the more embarrassed by
her friends' presence

Feeling empty
The Mountain's daughter

turned to go home
It was hard

76.

Into his arms the Mountain took
his pitiful daughter

Eye-buds shut
Afraid of terrible Śiva

He took the road back
Steps stretching in haste

Like the elephant-king carrying
a lotus clinging to his tusk

END OF CANTO III

from

MĀLAVIKĀGNIMITRAM

Mālavikā and Agnimitra

Mālavikāgnimitram is a romantic comedy about King Agnimitra's love for his chief queen Dhāriṇī's maid, Mālavikā, who turns out to be a princess. Agnimitra falls in love with a portrait of Mālavikā, and his jester-friend Gautama sets up a dance competition where Agnimitra can see Mālavikā in person. Mālavikā too falls in love with the king. The next act has revelations. Summoned by junior queen Irāvatī, a disinterested Agnimitra goes to a meeting place in a garden. He finds Mālavikā there in a love-struck state, hides, and spies on her. Mālavikā has come here to help Dhāriṇī in a ritual. A young woman's kick can help an Aśoka tree blossom, and if the Aśoka tree responds to Mālavikā's kick, Dhāriṇī will grant Mālavikā her heart's desire. Meanwhile, Irāvatī arrives, and on seeing Mālavikā, hides too. Mālavikā's friend lets her know that the king is smitten with her; Mālavikā is pleased. The king jumps out of hiding to declare his love, and a furious Irāvatī also jumps out of hiding. The king tries to placate her, in vain. Then, incited by Irāvatī, Dhāriṇī imprisons Mālavikā. In the hilarious Act IV excerpted here, Gautama plots to help Mālavikā escape from prison for a rendezvous with Agnimitra. The lovers meet in a beach house, and again, they are found out. It all ends well: the Aśoka tree blooms, Mālavikā is really a princess, and Dhāriṇī consents to Agnimitra's marriage with Mālavikā.

Interwoven through the romantic plot is a war that is taking place off-stage. Agnimitra is the king of Vidiśā. Before the play opens, he has captured the brother-in-law of Yajñasena, the king of Vidarbha, who retaliates by kidnapping Agnimitra's cousin Mādhavasena. In Act I of the play, Agnimitra orders a military onslaught against Vidarbha. In Act V, Agnimitra has won this war, and as a tribute, receives two singers who recognize Mālavikā as a princess. A nun in Dhāriṇī's retinue reveals herself as the wife of one of the deceased commanders of Mādhavasena, confirms Mālavikā's identity as Mādhavasena's sister, and shares a prophecy that Mālavikā had to serve as a slave for a year before finding a suitable husband.

One of Kālidāsa's themes is that of the blurred line between reality and representation, and the power of imagination to conjure reality. Just as Agnimitra responds to the painting of Mālavikā, in Act IV, Mālavikā responds to a portrait of Agnimitra, mistaking the portrait for Agnimitra. This is strongly reminiscent of a scene in *Śākuntalam* where a lovelorn Duṣyanta gazes at a painting of Śakuntalā, mistaking it for Śakuntalā in person. Women characters dominate the play, and we see more of the domestic side of a king's life. Dhāriṇī's status is acknowledged by other characters. As the king's chief queen she is equated with the Earth, but has to maintain her status in a polygamous situation, and she does so with pragmaticism and dignity—she keeps her promise to Mālavikā without complaint. By contrast, junior queen Irāvatī is rash, and portrayed as unreasonably jealous. Gautama's role as court jester is also similar to that of Mādhavya in *Śākuntalam*—friend to the king, cunning and savvy, but clownish. He is also a caricature of a brahmin: more keen on good food than aesthetic appreciation, and so nervous that he mistakes a stick for a snake.

The actions of the plot suggest that Agnimitra is more comic than heroic. Unlike Duṣyanta of *Śākuntalam*, or Purūravas of *Vikramorvaśīyam*, who engage in battles and rescue missions, Agnimitra is nervous about the displeasure of his queens and busies himself with spying on Mālavikā in the beach house as a war occurs off-stage. But Agnimitra's statecraft and political acumen come across in his responses and decisions, when he receives a message about the King of Vidarbha's offensive in Act I, and in Act V, when he receives a letter from his General that a sacrifice has been interrupted by Greek soldiers. It is also this context of war and unrest at the borders that provides some historical information. Scholars link the hero to King Agnimitra of the Śuṅga dynasty of the second century BCE.

CAST OF CHARACTERS

AGNIMITRA: The king

DHĀRIṆĪ: Agnimitra's chief queen

IRĀVATĪ: Agnimitra's junior queen

MĀLAVIKĀ: Agnimitra's lover; the princess of Vidarbha, disguised as a maid in Dhāriṇī's retinue.

GAUTAMA: Court jester and the king's childhood friend

VĀHATAKA: Chief Minister

BAKULĀVALIKĀ: Mālavikā's friend

MĀDHAVIKĀ: Prison guard

JAYASENĀ: The king's attendant

ASCETIC WOMAN: The sister of the chief minister of Vidarbha, and Mālavikā's guardian, disguised as an ascetic woman in Dhāriṇī's retinue.

NIPUṆIKĀ: Irāvatī's attendant

NAGARIKĀ: Irāvatī's attendant

VASULAKṢMĪ: Child-princess

DHRUVASIDDHI: A doctor

ACT IV

(*The lovelorn King Agnimitra enters with attendant Jayasenā*)

AGNIMITRA: (*To himself*)

> Hope took root
> when I heard of her
>
> Passion burst blossoms
> when I saw her
>
> Sprouted goosebumps when
> my hand touched her
>
> May the tree of love make
> the taster of its fruit, me

(*Aloud*) Hey, Gautama!

JAYASENĀ: Gautama is not here.

AGNIMITRA: (*To himself*) I sent him to gain news of Mālavikā.

GAUTAMA: (*Enters*) Greetings, King!

AGNIMITRA: Jayasenā, inquire where Chief Queen Dhāriṇī is, how she's resting her twisted ankle.

JAYASENĀ: As you wish. (*Leaves*)

AGNIMITRA: Gautama, what news of Mālavikā?

GAUTAMA: Cuckoo, caught by a cat.

AGNIMITRA: (*Sadly*) How so?

GAUTAMA: The poor girl has been thrown into the underground prison by her, that red-eyed chief queen of yours.

AGNIMITRA: Did she find out about my rendezvous?

GAUTAMA: What else!

AGNIMITRA: Who's this who is against me and made the chief queen angry with me?

GAUTAMA: Listen King, the Ascetic Woman told me this. Yesterday, Junior Queen Irāvatī visited Chief Queen Dhāriṇī who has a sprained ankle, to ask after her health.

AGNIMITRA: And then?

GAUTAMA: Then Dhāriṇī asked her, did you see our beloved king? Irāvatī said, go slow on the endearments, don't you know about the rendezvous between our 'beloved' king and your maid?

AGNIMITRA: Even without particulars, it's obvious that the reference suspects Mālavikā. And then?

GAUTAMA: Then, pressed by Dhāriṇī, Irāvatī gave away information about your indiscretion.

AGNIMITRA: What deep fury she has! Say what happened next.

GAUTAMA: What next … Mālavikā and Bakulāvalikā experience life in hell, where even the sun cannot be seen, their feet bound up like snake-goddesses.

AGNIMITRA: Tough luck.

> A sweet-voiced cuckoo and bee
> Hanging out freely on a mango tree
>
> Now stuck in a hollow by untimely rain
> and a strong windstorm

Is there a way out of this mess?

GAUTAMA: How can there be? Mādhavikā, who prevails over the prison, has been instructed. 'Without seeing my signet ring, don't release the miserable Mālavikā and Bakulāvalikā.'

AGNIMITRA: (*Sighs, thoughtfully*) What's to be done in this situation, my friend?

GAUTAMA: (*Thinks*) There's a solution.

AGNIMITRA: What is it?

GAUTAMA: (*Looks around*) Someone we don't see will be listening. I'll whisper in your ear. (*Goes closer, informs the king*) Like that.

AGNIMITRA: (*Happily*) Nice! Use it for success!

(*Attendant Nipuṇikā enters*)

JAYASENĀ: King, Chief Queen Dhāriṇī relaxes on an outdoor chaise longue, feet being massaged with red sandalwood paste by her maid's hands, as the Ascetic Woman amuses her with stories.

AGNIMITRA: Then this is the right moment for me to visit her.

GAUTAMA: Go ahead, King. I will too, but not empty-handed.

AGNIMITRA: Do so after Jayasenā's been made aware of our secret.

GAUTAMA: As you say. (*Whispers in her ear*) It's like this. (*Leaves after informing Jayasenā*)

AGNIMITRA: Jayasenā, show me the way to the outdoor chaise longue.

JAYASENĀ: This way, this way, King.

(*Dhāriṇī on a chaise longue, Irāvatī, Ascetic Woman, Nagarikā and Nipuṇikā enter by rank*)

NIPUṆIKĀ: Ma'am, the story is charming. Do tell us what happens next.

ASCETIC WOMAN: (*Looks around*) Ma'am, I'll tell the rest later. Here's the King of Vidiśā.

DHĀRIṆĪ: It's my husband!

(*Wants to get up*)

AGNIMITRA: Don't, don't—no need for this polite gesture …

Sweet-spoken, don't,
Don't stress

your foot that usually
rests on gold pedestals

Now twisted

Already suffering
separation from anklets

And you mustn't
stress over me

DHĀRIṆĪ: May my husband win!

ASCETIC WOMAN: May the king succeed!

AGNIMITRA: (*Greets the ascetic woman and sits*) And, Queen, is the pain tolerable?

DHĀRIṆĪ: It is a bit better today.

(*Gautama enters, flustered, his thumb bandaged*)

GAUTAMA: Save me, save me, King! I've been bitten by a snake.

(*Everyone's upset*)

AGNIMITRA: Oh no. Where have you been wandering?

GAUTAMA: I thought I'd see the queen, so I went to the pleasure garden to gather appropriate flowers.

DHĀRIṆĪ: Oh no, I'm the one who's responsible for the risk to this brahmin's life.

GAUTAMA: For the Aśoka blossoms, I outstretched my hand. Then, was bitten by Death in the form of a snake that came out of a hollow. Here are the two fang-marks.

(*Shows the bites*)

ASCETIC WOMAN: Then, as it's advised, the first thing to do is slash the bite. Let that be done right away.

> Slashing the bite, amputation
> or blood-letting—these
>
> the lifesaving remedies
> for those bitten

AGNIMITRA: Now this is the work of a doctor. Jayasenā, quickly get Dhruvasiddhi.

JAYASENĀ: As you say. (*Leaves*)

GAUTAMA: Argh, I'm in the grip of evil Death.

AGNIMITRA: Don't be scared. Sometimes a bite can be poisonless.

GAUTAMA: How can I not be scared? My limbs tingle.

(*Mimes the onset of poison*)

DHĀRIṆĪ: (*Goes near Gautama*) The visible change does not augur well. Take care of the brahmin.

(*Attendants hold him up, flustered*)

GAUTAMA: (*Looks at the king*). Sir, I've been your close friend since your childhood. Consider that, take good care of my son-less mother.

AGNIMITRA: Gautama, don't be afraid. Stay calm. In no time, the doctor will treat you.

(*Jayasenā enters*)

JAYASENĀ: King, Dhruvasiddhi, who has been summoned, asks, 'Bring him, Gautama, here instead.'

AGNIMITRA: Then have the eunuch-attendant take him to the good doctor.

JAYASENĀ: Okay.

GAUTAMA: (*Looks at the queen*) Ma'am, whether I live or not, forgive me for any faults I may have in serving the king here.

DHĀRIṆĪ: May you live long.

(*Gautama and Jayasenā leave*)

AGNIMITRA: The poor fellow is timid by nature. He doesn't even have confidence in Dhruvasiddhi, aptly named 'constantly successful'.

(*Jayasenā enters*)

JAYASENĀ: King, Dhruvasiddhi said, 'I need something with the image of a snake to do the water-pitcher magic ritual. Find it.'

QUEEN: This is a ring with the seal of a snake. Return this to my hand later.

(*Gives the ring; Jayasenā takes it and starts to leave*)

AGNIMITRA: Jayasenā, when the job is done, bring the news to me quickly.

JAYASENĀ: As you say. (*Leaves*)

ASCETIC WOMAN: Even as my heart says it, Gautama is free from poison.

AGNIMITRA: May that be so.

(*Jayasenā re-enters*)

JAYASENĀ: King! Gautama is free from the effect of the poison and is back to normal already.

DHĀRIṆĪ: Luckily, I'm free from blame.

JAYASENĀ: And then, Minister Vāhataka sends a message, 'Many governmental matters to be discussed, I want the favour of seeing you.'

DHĀRIṆĪ: Go, husband, succeed at your work.

AGNIMITRA: Queen, the sun's heat fills this place. A coolant is the cure for your illness. Have the chaise longue moved elsewhere.

DHĀRIṆĪ: Girls, do as my husband says.

ATTENDANTS: Yes, of course.

(*Dhāriṇī, Irāvatī and their attendants leave*)

AGNIMITRA: Jayasenā, lead me to the pleasure garden by a secret route.

JAYASENĀ: This way, King, this way.

AGNIMITRA: Jayasenā, I suppose Gautama got the job done?

JAYASENĀ: But of course.

AGNIMITRA:

I believe the plan
for the desired date's

sure to succeed
Yet my timid heart

Doubtful
Uncertain

(*Gautama enters*)

GAUTAMA: Hello, King. Your work is done.

AGNIMITRA: Jayasenā, you can do your own thing now.

JAYASENĀ: As you wish. (*Leaves*)

AGNIMITRA: Gautama, Mādhavikā seems stupid, no questions from her?

GAUTAMA: Seeing the queen's signet-ring, how could she have questions?

AGNIMITRA: I'm not talking about the signet-ring. She ought to ask these kinds of questions: 'How come these two are being released?' 'Why did the queen send you rather than her own attendants?'

GAUTAMA: Yes, I was interrogated. Although I'm a dunce-head, in this particular case, my wits were present.

AGNIMITRA: Do tell!

GAUTAMA: I said—'The king was told by astrologers, "Your stars are in a bad position. Therefore, release all prisoners."'

AGNIMITRA: (*Happily*) And then?

GAUTAMA: Hearing that, Dhāriṇī, out of politeness for the opinion of Irāvatī who was there, asked me to release Mālavikā under the authority of the king. She said, 'It's appropriate.' Thus the job was actually achieved by way of her.

AGNIMITRA: (*Hugs the jester*) I'm much closer to you now!

> A friend's interests, not
> gained by wits alone
>
> Empathy too, the way to
> a successful mission

GAUTAMA: Hurry. I put Mālavikā with her friend in the beach house, and then came to see you.

AGNIMITRA: I'll give her my attention. You lead.

GAUTAMA: Come, King. (*Walks around*) This is the beach house.

AGNIMITRA: (*Suspiciously*) Irāvatī's maid Candrikā approaches, hands busy gathering flowers. We'll hide ourselves behind this wall then.

GAUTAMA: Yes indeed! Thieves and lovers must avoid Candrikā the moonlight!

(*Both do as they say*)

AGNIMITRA: Gautama, how does your friend wait for me? Let's look through this window.

GAUTAMA: Okay.

(*Both stand, looking*)

(*Enter Mālavikā and Bakulāvalikā*)

BAKULĀVALIKĀ: Greet your husband, friend!

MĀLAVIKĀ: Namaste.

AGNIMITRA: I suspect she's pointing to my portrait.

MĀLAVIKĀ: (*Happily*) Thank you! (*Looks at the door, sadly*) You fool me!

AGNIMITRA: I'm pleased by the lady's joy and sadness, both.

> A lotus at sunrise
> or at sunset?
>
> This pretty-face's face
> Contrary at once

BAKULĀVALIKĀ: In fact, this is the king's portrait.

MĀLAVIKĀ AND BAKULĀVALIKĀ: (*Bow to the portrait*) Greetings, King.

MĀLAVIKĀ: Just as I didn't feel as much longing for him then when I saw him in a hurry, now I experience the portrait full of desire.

GAUTAMA: Did you hear? The lady there says, 'He doesn't look like his portrait.' You're a fool, carting around the pride of your youth like a casket of jewels.

AGNIMITRA: Women are modest even when they're interested. See:

> They want to study
> the form of the lover
>
> Eager-eyed, to
> take it all in
>
> But when they first meet
> their lovers, their eyes
>
> don't go there

MĀLAVIKĀ: Friend, who is this my husband looks at, sidelong, softly?

BAKULĀVALIKĀ: That is Irāvatī to his side.

MĀLAVIKĀ: He seems impolite, gaze directed at just one spot, leaving all the other queens…

BAKULĀVALIKĀ: (*To herself*) She's jealous, imagining the portrait of her husband as real. Fine. I'll play with her. (*Aloud*) Irāvatī's the king's sweetheart.

MĀLAVIKĀ: Then why should I take the trouble… (*Turns away in jealousy*)

AGNIMITRA: Look!

> Face turned away
> from the portrait
>
> in jealousy
> Lower lip throbs
>
> Knitted eyebrows smudge
> her forehead-dot

As if she demonstrates her
training in dramaturgy

Lovely. 'Anger
at a lover's offence'

GAUTAMA: Now be prepared to placate her.

MĀLAVIKĀ: And Gautama seems to serve him here too.

(*Again, she wants to face elsewhere*)

BAKULĀVALIKĀ: (*Blocks Mālavikā*) Now, you're not angry, are you?

MĀLAVIKĀ: If you think I'm angry for too long, I'll take back my anger.

AGNIMITRA: (*Approaches*)

How come, water-lily eyes
You're peeved at my ways

in a portrait! Here I am
in person, your love-slave

Dedicated to no other

BAKULĀVALIKĀ: Oh the king! Welcome!

MĀLAVIKĀ: (*To herself*) How was I made jealous by my husband's portrait! (*Visibly blushing as she greets him*)

(*The king mimes awkwardness from love*)

GAUTAMA: Why do you look indifferent?

AGNIMITRA: From not trusting her.

GAUTAMA: Distrust this lady? How so?

AGNIMITRA: Listen.

Your friend,

In dreams before my eyes
Then gone in seconds

Though between my arms
Abruptly slips away

My friend,

How can my heart
be sure of her?

The mirage of her visits
Love's wounds

BAKULĀVALIKĀ: You've given the king the slip many times. Make yourself trustworthy now.

MĀLAVIKĀ: Unlucky as I am, even love with him in dreams has become rare.

BAKULĀVALIKĀ: Please respond to her, King.

AGNIMITRA:

Why answer when
my very being's given

to your friend?
Witnessed by the fire

of love, five-arrowed
Kāma, in secret,

I'm not her master
But her servant

BAKULĀVALIKĀ: I'm honoured.

GAUTAMA: (*Walks about in a hurry*) Oh Bakulāvalikā, this deer tramples a young Aśoka tree's leaves. Come, let's go check. (*Starts to leave*)

BAKULĀVALIKĀ: Ah so.

AGNIMITRA: You should be right here, to guard us.

GAUTAMA: Does Gautama need to be told that too?

BAKULĀVALIKĀ: (*Walks around*) Gautama, I'll remain hidden. You be the door-guard.

GAUTAMA: That's right.

(*Bakulāvalikā leaves*)

GAUTAMA: Then I'll stay on this marble platform. (*Does so*) Nice to the touch! (*Falls asleep*)

(*Mālavikā waits, shy*)

AGNIMITRA:

> Hey pretty one, drop your
> fear of making love
>
> to me, longing for love
> for a long time
>
> Like the Atimukta vine,
> Cling to me, a mango tree

MĀLAVIKĀ: From fear of the queen, I'm unable to do what's pleasing to me.

AGNIMITRA: Don't be afraid.

MĀLAVIKĀ: (*Smiles*) He who does not fear, I've seen him when he met Junior Queen Irāvatī.

AGNIMITRA:

O Bimba-fruit-red lips!

Politeness is the norm
in the Bimbaka clan

Thus, elegant-eyes,
Whatever life's left

in me, that depends
on hope for you

Then accept me, a man who's been longing for you for so long. (*Embraces her tightly*)

(*Mālavikā mimes an effort to avoid him*)

AGNIMITRA: (*To himself*) Charming how young women express love. So, here:

Herself trembling, she blocks my hand
My restless fingers try to go below

Takes her hands to cover her breasts
As I forcefully embrace her

Turns her face away as I lift it
to drink in her long-lashed eyes

(*Irāvatī and Nipuṇikā enter*)

IRĀVATĪ: Hey Nipuṇikā, are you sure you understood Candrikā right? Gautama was seen sleeping alone in the verandah of the beach house?

NIPUṆIKĀ: Or else how could I inform you?

IRĀVATĪ: Then let's go there. Let's go to ask after our dear friend who's free from danger.

NIPUṆIKĀ: Something remains to be said in the queen's words…

IRĀVATĪ: Also, to please the king's portrait.

NIPUṆIKĀ: Then why don't you suck up to the king himself in person?

IRĀVATĪ: Fool! He's as unresponsive in person as he is in his portrait. My husband's heart has moved on to someone else. This effort is just a way to apologize for me overstepping my bounds.

NIPUṆIKĀ: This way, Queen, this way.

(*Both walk about*)

(*Maid Nagarikā enters*)

NAGARIKĀ: Greetings, Queen. Chief Queen says, 'This is not the time to be spiteful. It is out of regard for you that I confined Mālavikā and her maid to prison. If you agree, I'll do what our husband the king wants. Let me know.'

IRĀVATĪ: Nagarikā, tell the chief queen—'Who am I to instruct the chief queen? Your favour to me was evident in punishing the maid Mālavikā. By whose grace but hers do I thrive?'

NAGARIKĀ: Okay. (*Leaves*)

NIPUṆIKĀ: (*Walks about, looks around*) Queen! Here's Gautama, asleep while sitting at the door of the beach house, like a bull gone to a bazaar.

IRĀVATĪ: Oh no. Not a turn for the worse because of poison that remains!

NIPUṆIKĀ: His complexion seems fine. And he was treated by Dhruvasiddhi. It's wrong to be concerned.

GAUTAMA: (*Talks in his dream*) Oh, good Mālavikā!

NIPUṆIKĀ: Did you hear that, Queen! Whose son is this rascal, and to whom is he partial? All this while, stuffed his tummy with dumplings in return for blessings, now he dreams about Mālavikā!

GAUTAMA: May you trump Irāvatī.

NIPUṆIKĀ: This is too much. I'll scare this snake-fearing so-called brahmin by throwing this stick that's crooked as a snake, while hiding behind this pillar.

IRĀVATĪ: This ingrate deserves to be rattled.

(*Nipuṇikā throws a stick at Gautama*)

GAUTAMA: (*Wakes up suddenly*) Hell! Hell! Hey King! A snake has fallen on me!

AGNIMITRA: (*Approaches at once*) My friend, don't be scared.

MĀLAVIKĀ: (*Follows*) Husband, don't go there so abruptly, he says it's a snake.

IRĀVATĪ: (*Runs*) Oh no! Oh no! My husband is rushing in our direction.

GAUTAMA: (*Laughs*) This is a stick, how come. I thought, since I blamed a snake, when I was actually pierced with a Ketaka thorn, this must be the result.

(*Throwing aside the curtain, Bakulāvalikā enters*)

BAKULĀVALIKĀ: Don't enter, King. It looks like a snake with a crooked gait here.

IRĀVATĪ: (*From behind the pillar, approaches the king suddenly*) Has today's date been amusing, without any interruption?

(*Upon seeing Irāvatī, everyone's confused*)

AGNIMITRA: My love, this courtesy is rather irregular.

IRĀVATĪ: Bakulāvalikā, luckily, your effort to be a go-between for a rendezvous is complete.

BAKULĀVALIKĀ: Be happy, Queen. God must ask why I did so. Does God forget to rain on the earth just because the frogs croak?

GAUTAMA: Don't be like that. Just by seeing you, the king here has forgotten your impoliteness. But again, even today, you don't please him.

IRĀVATĪ: I'm angry now, what can I do?

AGNIMITRA: This anger is out of place, it does not suit you.

> Lovely one, when
> did you, hey,
>
> without reason,
> get this angry role
> in a flash? Say,
>
> can a moon's orb
> eclipse on the
> wrong night?

IRĀVATĪ: 'Without reason.' Well said, husband. If I should be angry again when my good luck has moved on to another, then I would be ridiculous.

AGNIMITRA: You're imagining something else. I repeat, I really don't see any place for anger.

> Servants don't deserve to be in jail
> on festival days, even if guilty
>
> It's why they were released, and why
> they came to me, to fall at my feet

IRĀVATĪ: Nipuṇikā, go, tell the chief queen, 'I've seen your partiality to me today.'

NIPUṆIKĀ: Okay. (*Leaves*)

GAUTAMA: Disaster. The home-pigeon that was released from the cage has fallen at the sight of a cat.

NIPUṆIKĀ: (*Aside*) I happened to run into Mādhavikā who told me, this is how it has been set up. (*Whispers in Irāvatī's ear*)

IRĀVATĪ: (*To herself*) Possible. Really, this idea here was set up by the so-called brahmin. (*Looks at Gautama, aloud*) This is the politics of the minister of love-sciences.

GAUTAMA: Ma'am, if I've even studied one syllable of politics, then the Gāyatrī mantra would be forgotten by me.

AGNIMITRA: (*To himself*) How can I get out of this spot?

(*Jayasenā enters*)

ATTENDANT: King! Princess Vasulakṣmī, running after a ball, was scared stiff by a red-faced monkey. She's sitting on the queen's lap, trembling like a leaf in the wind, is almost senseless.

AGNIMITRA: A problem. Childhood is so fragile.

IRĀVATĪ: (*Excited*) Hurry, husband, to console her. Don't let the effect of her shock get worse.

AGNIMITRA: I'll bring her back to consciousness. (*Walks away in a hurry*)

GAUTAMA: (*To himself*) Well done, red-faced monkey, well done. You've saved your own side from a tight spot.

(*Agnimitra, Gautama, Irāvatī, Nipuṇikā and the attendant leave*)

MĀLAVIKĀ: My friend, my heart shudders when I think of the queen. I don't know what else remains to be endured after this.

VOICE BACKSTAGE: Surprise, surprise! Although five nights of doing the 'dohada' ritual are not over, the golden Aśoka is full of buds. I'll let the queen know.

(*Both listen with joy*)

BAKULĀVALIKĀ: Console yourself, my friend. The queen is true to her word.

MĀLAVIKĀ: Then I'll follow the keeper of the pleasure garden.

BAKULĀVALIKĀ: Okay.

(*They leave*)

END OF ACT IV

from

VIKRAMORVAŚĪYAM

Heroism Wins Urvaśī

A five-act play about a poignant and complicated love between a mortal and an apsarā, *Vikramorvaśīyam* is set in the legendary past, and fragments of the story can be found in hymn 10.95 of the *Ṛgveda*. When the beautiful apsarā Urvaśī is kidnapped by a demon, King Purūravas rescues her, and they fall in love with each other. Urvaśī returns to svarga (heaven) where she usually lives under the domain of the chief god Indra and performs music and dance in the assembly of the gods. Purūravas returns to his kingdom on Earth. Act II, translated here, is delightful for romantic intrigue; in Act II, Purūravas muses over Urvaśī's beauty to his friend, the jester Māṇavaka. Deciding to follow up on the encounter, Urvaśī comes to Earth along with her friend Citralekhā. Using her powers of invisibility, she eavesdrops on Purūravas and then responds to his confessions with a love letter on a birch leaf. When she finally reveals herself, the lovers are unable to get closer as Urvaśī is asked to return to svarga for a performance. A distracted Purūravas hands over the letter for safekeeping to Māṇavaka, who promptly loses it. Queen Auśīnarī on the lookout for her husband Purūravas, finds the birch-leaf love letter. A sheepish Purūravas apologizes, Auśīnarī stomps off. Back in svarga, Urvaśī mistakenly utters the name 'Purūravas' instead of 'Puruṣottama' in the lyrics of her performance, and she is fired from her celestial position. Mitigating the punishment, Indra says she may live with Purūravas, but only until the face of the child born to them is seen by Purūravas. Urvaśī goes to Earth and has an extended romance with Purūravas. In the heat of a lovers' tiff, she enters the forest of Kumāra, which is forbidden to women, and gets metamorphosed into a vine. A prolonged lamentation by Purūravas follows in Act IV, as he searches for her hopelessly, imagining her in every object. A magical gem helps restore Urvaśī's form, and the lovers are reunited. In Act V, Purūravas discovers he has a son, and meets him; prophecy fulfilled, Urvaśī prepares to return to svarga. The gloom is interrupted by Indra's messenger who asks Purūravas for help in a battle with demons in return for Urvaśī's companionship on Earth until the end of his life.

Like the other two Kālidāsa plays, *Vikramorvaśīyam* also focuses on a king's romance, and there is comic tension in the contrast between his bravado as a lover and his timidity as a husband. Unlike Duṣyanta and Agnimitra, Purūravas does not show much of his role as a king, but his valour is sought after by Indra, just like Duṣyanta's. Māṇavaka plays the well-fed, clownish brahmin, confidant of the king, and informant for the queen, though he is more naïve than the jesters of the other Kālidāsa plays. Urvaśī's charisma takes over Purūravas completely and also overshadows Queen Auśīnarī.

CAST OF CHARACTERS

PURŪRAVAS: The king

MĀṆAVAKA: Court jester; the king's childhood friend

URVAŚĪ: An apsarā; lover of Purūravas

CITRALEKHĀ: Urvaśī's friend

AUŚĪNARĪ: Purūravas's queen

NIPUṆIKĀ: Queen's maid

And some attendants for the queen's entourage

ACT II

MĀṆAVAKA, THE JESTER: Heh heh heh. Like someone invited to a feast of the finest food, I won't be able to control my tongue to protect the king's secret. Especially in a crowd. So, I'll hang about near the Vimānaparicchanda Mansion where there's less people, until the king gets off work. (*Walks about and stops*)

(*Nipuṇikā, a maid, enters*)

NIPUṆIKĀ: I've been ordered by the queen, daughter of the King of Kāśī. 'Nipuṇikā, since the king came back from worshipping the Sun, he seems vacant. Find out, then, from his close friend Māṇavaka, why he's upset.' But then, how can I fool that so-called brahmin? Or maybe, like a dewdrop at the tip of a blade of grass, about to fall, the king's secret won't keep too long. I'll look for him then. (*Walks around, looking*) There's Māṇavaka, gone all silent, weird, like a monkey in a painting. I'll approach him then. (*Goes near*) Hello, Sir.

MĀṆAVAKA: Be well, Miss. (*To himself*) Seeing this rascal maid, it's as if the king's secret bursts out of my heart. Hey Nipuṇikā, where are you going, leaving your music lessons?

NIPUṆIKĀ: To see you, by the queen's orders.

MĀṆAVAKA: What does the lady want?

NIPUṆIKĀ: The queen says, 'Māṇavaka is always on my side, he won't ignore me when I'm so badly distressed.'

MĀṆAVAKA: (*Measuredly*) Did my friend, the king, behave inappropriately with the queen?

NIPUṆIKĀ: Sir, the king addressed the queen by the name of the woman for whom he pines.

MĀṆAVAKA: (*To himself*) Well, the king himself has given away his secret. Then why do I suffer, now, forcibly, with my tongue? (*Aloud*)

Was she called 'Urvaśī'? The sight of that apsarā makes the obsessed king annoy not just the queen, but me too; he's turned away from all entertainment!

NIPUṆIKĀ: (*To herself*) I've broken the king's wall of secrecy. (*Aloud*) Sir, what shall I tell the queen then?

MĀṆAVAKA: Nipuṇikā, inform the queen that I'll try to make him drop that fantasy. Only then will I show my face to the queen.

NIPUṆIKĀ: As you say. (*Leaves*)

A SINGER, BACKSTAGE:

> We think your job's like
> the sun's, and your power
>
> Dispels dark error
> in people worldwide
>
> The sun pauses for a moment
> in the middle of the sky
>
> So do you, in the day's sixth
> phase, to do what you like

MĀṆAVAKA: (*Listens*) The king gets up from his seat of duty and comes this way. I'll be at his side then. (*Leaves*)

(*The lovelorn Purūravas and Māṇavaka enter*)

> From the very first sight
>
> The lovely celestial lady's
> entered my heart
>
> The way to my heart was forged
> by fish-bannered Kāma's arrow
>
> Good shot!

MĀṆAVAKA: (*To himself*) No wonder he annoys the King of Kāśī's daughter, the queen.

PURŪRAVAS: And did you keep the secret I entrusted to you?

MĀṆAVAKA: (*Sadly, to himself*) Oh no, I've been fooled by that rascal maid. Or my friend would not probe me this way.

PURŪRAVAS: (*Doubtfully*) Why are you silent?

MĀṆAVAKA: I've held my tongue so much that I'm unable to respond to you all of a sudden.

PURŪRAVAS: Fine. Where shall we go now for entertainment?

MĀṆAVAKA: We'll go to the kitchen.

PURŪRAVAS: Why there?

MĀṆAVAKA: We could lift our low spirits by watching the lining up of ingredients and the prep of five kinds of food.

PURŪRAVAS: (*Smiles*) You'll be amused, being near your favourite things. How am I to amuse myself, when my prayer's unattainable?

MĀṆAVAKA: Have you come into Urvaśī's field of vision?

PURŪRAVAS: What if?

MĀṆAVAKA: Then I don't think she's hard to get.

PURŪRAVAS: You think so because you are fond of me.

MĀṆAVAKA: Your talk makes me curious. Is Urvaśī as unbeatable in beauty as I am in ugliness?

PURŪRAVAS: Māṇavaka, I can't describe every limb of hers. In brief, listen.

MĀṆAVAKA: I'm attentive.

PURŪRAVAS:

Her beauty's

An ornament for
ornaments

A highlight among
beautifications

A benchmark for all
similes

MĀṆAVAKA: It seems you've taken the vow of the Cātaka bird, desiring a celestial drink [*for the Cātaka bird subsists only on raindrops*].

PURŪRAVAS: There's no other refuge for one who's bereft. Show me the way to the pleasure garden.

MĀṆAVAKA: (*To himself*) What a fate. (*Aloud, walks about*) This way, King, this way. As if prompted by the pleasure garden, the south wind rises to welcome you.

PURŪRAVAS: The wind's name is apt—'southerliness' [*Dakṣiṇa*], a pun on 'courtesy' [*dākṣiṇya*].

Like a lover making

The Mādhavī vine wet
[Urvaśī]
The Kunda creeper dance
[The queen?]

Seems to me the combination
Of love and courtesy

MĀṆAVAKA: Let your drive be similar. This is the gate to the pleasure garden. Enter, King.

PURŪRAVAS: You go in first. (*Both enter*)

PURŪRAVAS: (*Looks ahead*) My guess was wrong, that just entering the pleasure garden would take away my gloom.

That I rushed, keen

To enter the garden
To cool my passion

Like one swept away
by a current, trying

To swim against it

MĀṆAVAKA: How so?

PURŪRAVAS:

First, irrepressible desire
for this hard-to-get object

Five-arrowed Kāma
My heart's devastated

What'll be my state
when the buds of

the garden mango tree
are bared

when the wind off Mt. Malaya blows
the dry leaves away

MĀṆAVAKA: Enough of this complaining. Soon Kāma himself will make you happy, fulfilling your desire.

PURŪRAVAS: I'll take the brahmin's word for it!

(*Both walk about*)

MĀṆAVAKA: See, King, the pleasure garden's loveliness points to springtime.

PURŪRAVAS: Sure I notice it at every step. Here:

> Kurabaka flowers ahead
> A woman's nails
>
> Rosy gleam
> Shadowed sides
>
> Young Aśoka's nice
> Red and ready
>
> to burst, face
> arched up
>
> New flower clusters
> on a mango tree
>
> Fringes burnished from
> sticky stamens' pollen
>
> Like lovely Spring—at a time
> between innocence and youth

MĀṆAVAKA: This Jasmine-vine bower with a marble seat seems as if personally seeking your favour, offering flowers dropped by bee-collisions. Be nice to it then…

PURŪRAVAS: As you please.

(*Both walk about and sit*)

MĀṆAVAKA: Here, comfortably seated, eyes drawn to pretty vines, cheer the lovesickness that comes from Urvaśī.

PURŪRAVAS: (*Sighs*)

> Not the freshly blossomed
> garden vines, nor the
> drooping trees
>
> Having seen her form
> My eyes have become
> hard-to-please

So think of an idea to make my prayers successful.

MĀṆAVAKA: (*Laughs*) The doctor who's supposed to treat Indra—who wanted Ahalyā—and I, supposed to treat you who wants Urvaśī, we're both crazy.

PURŪRAVAS: Don't say that. Strong friendship might show you how to do this.

MĀṆAVAKA: I'll think about it. Don't disturb my musing with your complaints. (*Thinks deeply*)

PURŪRAVAS: (*Senses an omen, says to himself*)

> She's not easy
> Full-moon face
> And yet this …
>
> My heart stops abrupt
> as if facing … reaching
> what's desired
>
> Kāma's handiwork?

(*Stays hopeful*)

(*Urvaśī and Citralekhā enter by air*)

CITRALEKHĀ: Where are you going, without saying where to?

URVAŚĪ: You mocked me then when I was sky-travelling and paused for a moment in the Himālaya near a vine—[*when my necklace was entangled*]. Why do you question me now?

CITRALEKHĀ: Oh, are you going to King Purūravas?

URVAŚĪ: Yes, that's exactly my errand, shame thrown to the wind!

CITRALEKHĀ: Whom did you send as go-between?

URVAŚĪ: My heart.

CITRALEKHĀ: Then you must think well of yourself.

URVAŚĪ: It's Kāma himself who prompts me. What's there to consider?

CITRALEKHĀ: To that, I have no answer.

URVAŚĪ: Then show me a way where there are no obstacles.

CITRALEKHĀ: Be confident. We've been put out of the reach of the enemies of the gods by the guru of the gods, who also taught us how to tie our hair in a knot called Aparājitā, or unbeatable.

URVAŚĪ: My mind forgot.

CITRALEKHĀ: We've arrived here at the king's palace, the jewel in the crown of Pratiṣṭha, as if looking at itself mirrored in the confluence of the sacred waters of the Gaṅgā and Yamunā.

URVAŚĪ: (*Looks*) It ought to be called 'the new address of heaven'. Friend, where might he be, who feels for the distressed?

CITRALEKHĀ: We'll find out by descending to this pleasure garden, that looks like a spot in the Nandana gardens [*of heaven*].

(*Both descend*)

CITRALEKHĀ: (*Sees the king, says happily*) Hey friend, here he is, expecting you, like the newly risen moon-god expects moonlight.

URVAŚĪ: (*Looks*) The king seems more attractive than when I first saw him.

CITRALEKHĀ: That's how it is. Then come. Let's go closer.

URVAŚĪ: Cloaked by the magic spell of Tiraskāriṇī, I'll go near him and listen. He stands there, alone, turned to his friend near him, saying something.

CITRALEKHĀ: As you please.

MĀṆAVAKA: I've thought of an idea for making love with your unreachable lover.

(*Purūravas remains silent*)

URVAŚĪ: Who's that woman the king prays for, who denies herself?

CITRALEKHĀ: Now, now, why do you behave like a human being?

URVAŚĪ: By my power, knowing what it is to be human, I'm suddenly afraid.

MĀṆAVAKA: I say, I've found a solution.

PURŪRAVAS: Then tell.

MĀṆAVAKA: Turn to sleep that lets you mate in a dream. Or, paint a picture of Urvaśī, and stay staring at it.

URVAŚĪ: (*Laughs, speaks to herself*) Petty-minded, be relieved!

PURŪRAVAS: Both are no good.

> How can I find sleep
> The creator of love-dreams
>
> This heart's ever-pierced
> by Kāma's arrows
>
> Nor can I see, for my eyes
> well up with tears
>
> Even before I finish drawing
> my darling Pretty-face

CITRALEKHĀ: Urvaśī, did you hear that?

URVAŚĪ: I did. But it's not enough for my heart.

MĀṆAVAKA: My brain only goes this far.

PURŪRAVAS: (*Sighs*)

> She doesn't know
> The intense pain of
> My broken heart
>
> Or knows my love
> by her power but
> mocks me
>
> My desire to love her
> Unfulfilled, fruitless.
> Be happy, Kāma

CITRALEKHĀ: Did you hear that?

URVAŚĪ: Oh, that he misunderstands me like this. I'm unable to confront him and answer. Instead I want to create a birch leaf with my power and put my answer there.

CITRALEKHĀ: You have my approval!

(*Urvaśī, in a fluster, holds a leaf, and does as she says*)

MĀṆAVAKA: (*Looks*) Oh! What's this that's fallen in front of us, like the sloughed-off skin of a snake?

PURŪRAVAS: (*Notices*) This is a birch leaf with an inscription of letters.

MĀṆAVAKA: Is it not possible that fortuitously Urvaśī heard your declarations and left a letter indicating her reciprocal love?

PURŪRAVAS: There's no stopping wishes. (*Takes the leaf, reads it, says happily*) Your guess was right.

MĀṆAVAKA: Please, now, King. I want to hear what's written here.

URVAŚĪ: Good man, you seem well-mannered.

PURŪRAVAS: Listen. (*Reads aloud*)

> If I feel for you
> as you—
>
> Passionate
> Unaware
>
> —think
>
> How come even the breezes of the gardens of heaven
> Burn my body tossing on a bed of Pārijāta flowers?

URVAŚĪ: Now what will he say?

CITRALEKHĀ: His limbs, thin like a lotus stalk, have already spoken.

MĀṆAVAKA: You're consoled, luckily, like hungry me getting delicious sweets at rituals.

PURŪRAVAS: Why call it only a consolation?

> The comparable passion
> My darling said
>
> so charmingly
> on a leaf
>
> Feels like we've met
>
> My face with
> her face
>
> My raised eyelashes
> with her wine-eyes

URVAŚĪ: Now our love is equally shared.

PURŪRAVAS: The letters will be spoilt by the sweat of my fingers. Keep this—my darling's own writing.

MĀṆAVAKA: (*Takes it*) Now, after parading the flowers, your heart's desires, will Urvaśī go back on her word over the fruit?

URVAŚĪ: While I steady my heart that's nervous to go near him, you show yourself and say what's appropriate.

CITRALEKHĀ: Okay. (*Removes the invisibility cloak of Tiraskāriṇī, approaches the king*) Greetings, King.

PURŪRAVAS: (*Happily*) Welcome, Ma'am.

> Like Yamunā—once
> seen in the confluence
> —without Gaṅgā
>
> Without your friend you
> don't make me as happy
> as before

CITRALEKHĀ: Don't you see a range of clouds first, then the streaks of lightning?

MĀṆAVAKA: (*Aside*) It's not Urvaśī? But her close friend?

CITRALEKHĀ: Head bowed, Urvaśī says to the king…

PURŪRAVAS: What does she command?

CITRALEKHĀ: 'When I was harassed by the enemies of the gods, you, King, were my saviour. Suffering badly from the love that occurred when I saw you, I'm in need of your kindness once more.

PURŪRAVAS:

> You say lovely Urvaśī's
> interested …

Don't you see how
Purūravas pines?

This Love's longing,
mutual

Like two red-hot irons—
Time to meet

CITRALEKHĀ: (*Approaches Urvaśī*) Come on, girl. Seeing that Kāma is tougher on him than on you, I've become his messenger.

URVAŚĪ: (*Removes the invisibility spell of Tiraskāriṇī*) How little it takes for you to abandon me!

CITRALEKHĀ: I'll find out soon, who abandons whom. Meanwhile, follow social customs.

URVAŚĪ: (*Approaches the king, says shyly*) Greetings, King, may you be a winner!

PURŪRAVAS: Hey Lovely,

When you say 'win'—

A word you never said
to anyone else but Indra

I've already won

(*He takes her by the hand and seats her*)

MĀṆAVAKA: Ma'am, why don't you say hello to the king's dear friend, the brahmin?

(*Urvaśī smiles and greets him with folded hands*)

MĀṆAVAKA: Be well, Ma'aṃ!

VOICE BACKSTAGE: Citralekhā, Urvaśī, hurry.

> The storm-gods and
> guardians of the world
>
> wish to see today
> the charming drama
>
> of eight emotions
> Sage Bharata taught you

(*Everyone listens; Urvaśī mimes sadness*)

CITRALEKHĀ: Did you hear the announcement of the messenger of the gods? Take the king's leave.

URVAŚĪ: I'm speechless.

CITRALEKHĀ: King, Urvaśī is a dependent. Please let her leave so as not to offend the gods.

PURŪRAVAS: (*Steadies his words with difficulty*) I'm not someone who goes against your god's orders. You must remember me.

(*Mimes the sadness of separation; Urvaśī leaves with her friend*)

PURŪRAVAS: (*Sighs*) Feels as if my eyes are pointless.

MĀṆAVAKA: (*Wants to show the king the letter*) But it—oh no! (*Stops halfway, says to himself*) I was so struck by seeing Urvaśī, I didn't notice that the birch-leaf letter slipped from my hands.

PURŪRAVAS: What do you want to say?

MĀṆAVAKA: Don't be depressed, King. Urvaśī feels strongly about you, she won't shake off this passion.

PURŪRAVAS: My heart has the same hope. That's why, at her departure …

Not her own boss, but
Her heart's her own

As if she deposited
her heart in me

with her sighs with
her heaving breasts

MĀṆAVAKA: (*To himself*) My heart shudders right now, that the king will now say 'Bring the birch leaf'.

PURŪRAVAS: How shall I entertain my eyes now? (*Remembers*) Ah yes, bring that birch leaf.

MĀṆAVAKA: (*Mimes regret*) Oh no, it's nowhere to be seen! It's gone, like Urvaśī.

PURŪRAVAS: Careless in all things, a fool. Look for it!

MĀṆAVAKA: (*Gets up*) It's here, yes it's here. (*Mimes searching*)

(*The daughter of the King of Kāśī, Queen Auśīnarī, enters along with Nipuṇikā and others in her entourage*)

AUŚĪNARĪ: Nipuṇikā, is it true, what you said, that the king was seen entering the vine-bower with Māṇavaka?

NIPUṆIKĀ: Have I ever told the queen anything untrue?

AUŚĪNARĪ: In that case, from behind the vines, I'll listen to their secret conversations. Whether what you said is true, or not.

NIPUṆIKĀ: As you please.

AUŚĪNARĪ: (*Walks about*) Hey Nipuṇikā, what is this, like an old rag, brought this way by the south wind.

NIPUṆIKĀ: (*Examines it*) It's a birch leaf, as it turns, letters appear. It's stuck in your own anklets. (*Takes it*) How did that happen? Read it aloud!

AUŚĪNARĪ: You read it. Then if it is not unsuitable, I'll hear it.

NIPUṆIKĀ: (*Does so*) Queen, it seems the same old scandal. I guess it's an ode to the king from Urvaśī. It's come to our hands only due to the carelessness of Māṇavaka, surely.

AUŚĪNARĪ: Then, I'll be its reader.

(*Nipuṇikā reads aloud the letter*)

AUŚĪNARĪ: I'll see the apsarā-lover with this very idea. (*Goes towards the vine-bower with her entourage*)

MĀṆAVAKA: King, what is that seen fluttering in the wind, around the playground-mountain near the pleasure garden?

PURŪRAVAS: (*Gets up*) Oh South wind, friend of Springtime—

> Take it away, the pollen
> gathered from Vīrudhā flowers
> by Spring. For its smell.
>
> But why steal, pointlessly,
> a handwritten letter from
> my girlfriend?
>
> You know via Añjanā
> How lovesick people thrive
> on diversions like these
>
> [*Legend: The Wind-god*
> *blew on pretty Añjanā's skirts…*
> *Their son, Hanumān*]

NIPUṆIKĀ: A search goes on for this very thing.

AUŚĪNARĪ: I see.

MĀṆAVAKA: I was fooled by a peacock feather, the colour of a dry Kesara blossom.

PURŪRAVAS: It's all over now.

AUŚĪNARĪ: (*Approaches*) King, don't be upset. Here's the birch leaf.

PURŪRAVAS: (*Flustered*) Oh, Queen! Welcome!

MĀṆAVAKA: (*Aside*) Not 'well'-come at all, this outcome.

PURŪRAVAS: (*Aside*) What can we do now?

MĀṆAVAKA: Is there a solution for a thief caught with the booty?

PURŪRAVAS: (*Aside*) Idiot, this is no time for jokes. (*Aloud*) Queen, this is not what I'm looking for. We were looking for something quite different.

AUŚĪNARĪ: It's appropriate to hide your good luck!

MĀṆAVAKA: Ma'am, hurry with his meal. It will succeed in pacifying his overactive bile.

AUŚĪNARĪ: Nipuṇikā, nice, no, the brahmin helping his friend.

MĀṆAVAKA: Ma'am, see, even a devil will be pacified by a meal.

PURŪRAVAS: Fool, you're landing me in severe trouble.

AUŚĪNARĪ: You've not done anything wrong. I'm the one who is guilty, standing before you, as an unpleasant sight. I'll go from here. (*Mimes anger, and starts to leave*)

PURŪRAVAS: O' Plantain-thighs,

> I'm guilty
> Be happy
>
> Take a break from your anger
>
> When the Master's angered, how
> can the servant not be guilty?

(*Falls at her feet*)

AUŚĪNARĪ: (*To herself*) I'm not so naïve-at-heart that I'll accept his pleas. But I'm afraid I'll regret having acted ungraciously. (*Leaves the king, along with her entourage*)

MĀṆAVAKA: The queen's gone, like a river in the rains. Get up, then.

PURŪRAVAS: (*Gets up*) That was not inappropriate. See:

> Without true feeling, even
> a hundred loving words
>
> don't enter the hearts of wives
> to pacify them
>
> Just as a gem with fake colours,
> to those who know better

MĀṆAVAKA: This is quite convenient for you. One who has sore eyes can't stand the sight of a lamp.

PURŪRAVAS: Don't say that. Even though my heart's gone to Urvaśī, I think highly of the queen. But now that she has rejected my apology, I will rely on endurance.

MĀṆAVAKA: Let your endurance stay for a while. You're the support for a hungry brahmin. It's time to bathe and eat.

PURŪRAVAS: (*Looks up*) Half the day's gone.

(*Everyone leaves*)

> Suffering from heat the peacock sits
> in the cool basin around a tree-base
>
> The bee breaks open the bud
> of Karṇikāra and lies there

The flamingo abandons the hot lake
Goes to the lotus on the banks

Tired, in the pleasure-house,
the caged parrot asks for water

END OF ACT II

ABOUT THE TRANSLATOR

MANI RAO is the author of twelve books of poetry, including *So That You Know*. Her books in translation from Sanskrit include *Bhagavad Gita: God's Song* and *Saundarya Lahari: Wave of Beauty*. She researched mantra practices in tantric communities for *Living Mantra: Mantra, Deity and Visionary Experience Today*. Mani has an MFA in Creative Writing from UNLV, and a PhD in Religious Studies from Duke University, USA. She lives in Bangalore and Puttaparthi.

HarperCollins *Publishers* India

At HarperCollins India, we believe in telling the best stories and finding the widest readership for our books in every format possible. We started publishing in 1992; a great deal has changed since then, but what has remained constant is the passion with which our authors write their books, the love with which readers receive them, and the sheer joy and excitement that we as publishers feel in being a part of the publishing process.

Over the years, we've had the pleasure of publishing some of the finest writing from the subcontinent and around the world, including several award-winning titles and some of the biggest bestsellers in India's publishing history. But nothing has meant more to us than the fact that millions of people have read the books we published, and that somewhere, a book of ours might have made a difference.

As we look to the future, we go back to that one word—a word which has been a driving force for us all these years.

Read.